THE TROLL SOLUTION

THE TROLL SOLUTION

WEREWITCH™ BOOK EIGHT

RENÉE JAGGÉR

Bailey stood, leaning against the trunk of a century-old pine, and massaging her temples with the two forefingers of each hand. She had a headache.

"No," the tall guy with the soul patch insisted in his loud, sputtery voice, "you guys will just kill every single thing worth hunting in two weeks because your fat asses don't know how to cull, only practice genocide."

The other members of his pack laughed, but the werewolves in the opposing pack bristled and groaned.

"Bullshit!" the alpha of the opposition retorted. He was a shorter, muscular guy named George. "You dickheads don't know how to trust anyone, which is why you usually end up fucking things up along the exact lines that you're complaining about, and then you blame it on everyone else."

Bailey raised a hand. "Enough." She augmented the force and volume of her voice through magic so it echoed through the forest, and everyone fell silent. "Stop calling each other names. That's not going to get you anywhere. You can't negotiate worth a damn without a basic respect for the other guys. That goes for both of you."

The two packs turned to look at her, cowed by her intervention, but still tense and combative. They waited for her next pronouncement.

She stepped away from the trunk. "Okay, look. You already went to your damn shamans, and they suggested splitting the hunting grounds up half and half, but you started arguing over which half was better. *Then* they suggested that each of you would have the whole place for two weeks at a time before handing it over to the other pack, and you can't agree on that, either. So you've come to me to arbitrate."

She was Bailey "Nova" Nordin. Werewitch. High Shaman of the packs of North America, and the Pacific Northwest in particular, and most recently, newly-ascended goddess of both Weres and witches.

"So," she continued, "are you going to abide by my decision?"

Rumbles went around before the alphas barked, "Yes!" in virtual unison. It was nice to see them agree on *something*.

"Good." She looked around. "I hereby order you to switch the entire hunting grounds over to each other every single week, rather than every two weeks. That way, neither side will have enough time to deplete the game if you're worried about that, *and* you'll all get in the habit of knowing that the other guys will be using the woods again soon. Part of the deal is that you have to leave things in a decent state for the other pack. Do what I say and don't bitch about it. Try it out for a month or two, and you might be surprised at how good a job both of your packs end up doing."

There was a moment of awkward silence and some faint grumblings, but quickly enough, heads began to nod, men nudged each other, and the alphas agreed. They made a show of casting suspicious glares at their rivals. Of course. It was necessary to save face and look tough in front of their boys, but they seemed reasonably satisfied with her judgment.

"Okay," said the alpha with the soul patch, "fine, we can do that. As long as everyone doesn't over-hunt, the grounds should stay decent most of the time."

"Yeah," George agreed, "it should work, as long as everyone takes responsibility for their own actions."

Bailey nodded. "Right. Thanks for not arguing with me. Try not to fight among yourselves, either. There was a time when all of you guys would have died for each other against the Venatori, and that time was, what, two months ago? No point in being at each other's throats over something like this."

They agreed, nodding at her and filing off in their separate directions.

With the crowd of her people beginning to disperse in a state of what she hoped was lasting peace and contentment, Bailey wandered off separately from the rest of them. By herself, she went uphill. The forest thinned as she neared the mountain's summit, and when she found a reasonably flat place with a view of the landscape, she sat and rested.

An hour passed. Late afternoon turned to early

evening; dark was a ways off yet, but it would be twilight by the time she returned to Greenhearth. If she used conventional means of travel, anyway.

She had no pressing responsibilities, so she allowed the solitude of nature to recharge her spirit. In a way, arbitrating bullshit local disputes was more stressful and tiring than battling hostile gods.

As she was preparing to get up and descend back into the Hearth Valley to have a nice supper with Roland and her brothers, her ears, more sensitive than a wolf's, picked up the sounds of someone coming up the slope toward her.

Whoever they were, they were moving softly, making no excess noise, yet they weren't trying to hide their approach. It was the signature of someone who knew where he was going and was not worried about what he might find there.

She stood, turned, and waited. The figure that appeared in the shadows of the trees was someone she'd never seen before, an average-height white man with short black hair and a black beard, wearing brown-rimmed spectacles and a green jumpsuit.

"Hello," she said as he came closer and noticed her. "Can I help you? Or you just on a hike?"

The man stopped and smiled. "Good evening, Bailey. Yes, I've come to speak to you, but you probably suspected that, didn't you?"

The girl blinked. Hearing him speak and observing his mannerisms, she could have sworn she knew him, yet his face was not familiar.

"Okay," she replied. "Who are you, and what do you want to talk about?"

He glanced around, and she heard the sounds of someone else moving a bit farther down the mountain from them. Someone vacationing or getting exercise, or perhaps some of the Weres from the earlier crowd.

The man inclined his head toward the other side of the peak. "I'd like a moment of your time away from potentially prying eyes and ears. I'm sure you can understand that."

She gave a slow nod. "Yes." She started in the direction he'd indicated, cresting the peak and working her way down the other side toward a darker and less-used vale between four craggy hills.

The man followed her. She was suspicious but also confident in her powers, not to mention her prowess in using them. She'd survived many prior assassination attempts, and for the moment, she was not aware of any enemies who'd *want* to kill her.

They descended and found a shadowed nook beneath a cliff, surrounded by a dense growth of tall pines.

"Now, then," the man said softly, "we can dispense with the charade."

Bailey tensed as he waved his hand, but all that happened was a change in his appearance, as though someone had swapped out a camera lens and adjusted the focus.

The individual before her was the same height and slender build, but he was now dressed in an old dark coat, clean-shaven, and his green eyes were no longer covered by glasses. His black hair was shoulder-length, and a sly smirk played about his lips.

"Loki!" She crossed her arms over her chest. "What brings you out to see me? It's been a little while, hasn't it?"

His smile faded. "Longer than you think," he stated. "But yes." He glanced around and snapped his fingers, and a shimmering dome of transparent yellowish-green light surrounded them. Bailey assumed it was an anti-sound barrier.

Loki's eyes focused on her. "I'll cut right to the chase, dear girl. Fenris has been lying to you. In fact, he's been lying to *all* of us."

She stared blankly at him. It took five or six seconds before the magnitude of the statement struck her.

"What? How so?" The muscles along her jaw tightened. "And why the hell should I believe you? You're supposed to be the crafty-ass trickster who does crazy shit for fun. When you have a reputation like that, I'm gonna be skeptical of any bombshells you drop."

Loki sighed. "Yes, of course. I expected that, which is why I have plenty of evidence that you ought to consider. You might want to sit down."

"I'll stand," she insisted.

"So be it." He ran his thin fingers through his hair, then began his spiel.

"Since my son took you under his proverbial wing—or paw, whatever—look at everything that has happened. And *think*. Think logically about how *likely* some of it was to happen without outside interference. Without certain parties helping things to unfold in *just* such a way..."

The girl had known people who were suspicious and paranoid, people who found ways to connect any random spread of dots into a pattern they insisted was "logical." Still, she waited and allowed the god to speak.

"First," the trickster elaborated, "he appeared to you at the exact moment you were seeking a mentor to teach you the ways of shamanhood and how to be a proper were-witch. Also, he was the only one who contacted you, despite there being several other unattached shamans in the region. Curious, isn't it? Especially since he also appeared to you under false pretenses at first. I know all about this 'Marcus' persona of his, and so do you, yet you never pressed him on why he couldn't have revealed himself openly from the first."

She had to admit, that had always struck her as odd. But...

"He didn't want to attract attention," she retorted. "From the other gods, or the Venatori, or anyone like that."

"Oh, so he says," Loki quipped. "I suppose that would also explain why he was mysteriously unable to resolve disputes you found yourself engaged in, things of minor difficulty for him as the god of your people. Another shaman wanted you dead, and he stood back and watched? He could have intervened at any time to set things right. He is allowed that much under the covenant."

The girl considered. Her brain tried to come up with an explanation, something about letting her fight her own battles to gain experience, but before she could answer the charge, the trickster-god went on.

"Every step of your training, he has gone out of his way to help you and empower you. To raise you up as high as possible, even if it means putting you in severe danger or allowing bad things to happen that he could have prevented."

"Well," she responded, "isn't a good teacher *supposed* to challenge his students?"

Loki snorted. "This isn't what you think it is. It's not like he's given you a hard test and helped you study for it. It's more like he created a situation where it looks like the principal sexually harassed you or whatnot. Then he backed you up in suing the school—with his own lawyers specially chosen for the job in advance—so he could then place you on the school board and instruct you to elect a new principal he likes better. Something like that."

Tremors of fury went through Bailey's body. "What the fucking hell? Are you saying he's been *using* me? Were you there? Did you see everything we went through together? All the help he's given me? All the," a lump formed in her throat, "affection he's shown?"

Loki looked aside, into the darkness beneath the trees. When he turned back to the girl, he changed his approach.

"He means to start Ragnarök. You know what that is, don't you?"

"The end of the world, basically," she answered him. "What makes you say that? He's been cautious the whole time he's taught me. We did more together to *stop* the world from ending than anything. Where's your evidence?"

The trickster-god rubbed one eye with his left index finger. "He told me. He admitted to it."

The girl hadn't expected to hear that, but it wasn't as though Loki had produced a cell phone video to prove it.

"I don't know," Loki admitted, "exactly how he plans to go about it, or when he aims to bring it about, but it must be soon. You see, in order for Ragnarök to begin, a god must die. Specifically, a god of wolves must be sacrificed, and among our pantheon, there is only one individual who fits that bill—him. But..."

Bailey's gut clenched as she watched and listened. Loki's demeanor had grown more insinuating. For all that she balked at his words, it was impossible not to listen to them.

"...what if another deity were to rise to fill that role? What if he found a candidate whose trust he could earn, someone he could mold into a replacement to fulfill the terms of the prophecy while sparing himself?"

She felt sick, mostly because Loki would dare say such a thing.

But part of it was the possibility that if he was right, and telling the truth—unlikely though it was—the awfulness of it would all but destroy her. She refused to think about it too hard.

Loki was relentless, though.

"Look," he offered. He raised a hand and the light changed, forming an image somewhat like a hologram or a disembodied video screen—hazy at first, but growing more distinct. "Here I have visions of times I've found him acting according to his own rather odd purposes. I'm a master of illusion and trickery and so forth, so trailing anyone, even him, and spying on him without his knowledge is child's play for me. Look!"

The werewitch stared at the images in a near-trance.

Here was Fenris perched on a hilltop, watching her and Roland drive out of Greenhearth, and leaping through mountains to follow her. It was difficult to be certain, but she was pretty sure it was from before she'd met him in person, meaning that he'd been watching her before he'd introduced himself as Marcus.

Then the tall hooded man appeared again, this time going into an isolated cabin near a tall snowcapped peak in an area she didn't recognize; it was somewhere east of the Cascades, she suspected. There was an old man in the house. From a distance, it was hard to tell what happened, but she saw dark shapes move and heard brief screams and snarls and the thrashing and things being knocked over. Violence.

The next scene disturbed her far more than the previous two had. It showed Fenris standing next to Nick, the shaman from downstate who'd challenged her, as both of them looked over a scene of death and devastation, part of the Venatori's early rampage against the Were packs of Washington. As far as she'd known, Fenris and Nick had had nothing to do with one another.

Until Fenris had popped into the confrontation between him and Bailey and summarily executed the young shaman with a quick neck-snap before he could tell his side of the story.

There were scenes of Fenris watching her house at night, and of him observing her and Roland at times when she thought he'd been off on some important errand. Scenes of him sitting in strange places she'd never been to or seen, probably in the alternate arcane dimension known as the Other. These meant little to her, but there was something subtly *wrong* about them.

The final image Loki showed her was perhaps the most cryptic, yet it bothered her. It showed the interior of a room, dark but decorated with brightly-colored accouterments, with the shadows of a flickering fire being cast on the walls and door. Fenris walked into the frame of the picture, glancing back over his shoulder before opening the door and stepping outside.

The look on his face in that brief instant was unlike anything she'd seen from him—a cold, harsh, crazed look, the expression of a man who's done something he knows to be outrageous and is trying not to exult in it.

Loki snapped his fingers, and the images vanished.

Bailey looked up, and her eyes flashed. "How do I know that stuff is real? Since you're a master of illusions, you could have concocted all that shit out of thin air. There's no way to prove they were snapshots of what actually happened."

But it was impossible for her mind not to begin weaving the disparate threads into a pattern. Considering that Loki might be correct.

"I suppose not." He shrugged, his mouth in a flippant and sardonic twist. "But spend some time thinking it over. Go back and review all that's happened. See if everything adds up. I bet you'll find a handful of things that just...*don't.*"

I want to cry, Bailey admitted to herself. *I haven't done that in a long time, but I need to. Not here, and not now, but soon.*

"Fine." She grunted, giving no indication of how she felt within. "So, if all this *is* true, what am I supposed to do?"

He smiled. "Nothing...yet. Play along as though everything was the same, but be careful. Watch. *Observe.* Be ready, for when the time comes, we, the gods, will fall in by your side."

She glared at him. "If you're lying to me about this," she vowed, "I *will not* forget."

He started walking away. "Oh, I figured as much."

<hr>

Agents Velasquez and Park sat in front of an array of screens, watching and waiting as their software collated the pertinent data to create the time-lapse imagery they needed to tease out the necessary pattern.

Velasquez sighed. "Of all the fuckassery," he said through gritted teeth. "This is exactly the kind of shitstorm of shit Townsend used to rant about."

Park raised a finger. "Isn't he supposedly coming back on duty sometime soon? I heard guys in the lunchroom say that. Though of course, you can never trust what lunch-room guys say."

"I haven't heard anything," Velasquez countered, "one way or another. He might come back, or he might retire, or he might still die. I hope he does return since we could use his help, though he'll probably walk in, say 'Nope!' and walk straight back out when he sees *this* crap."

Using multiple pieces of the Agency's super-advanced tech, they had managed to match the energy signature of their target to dispersed masses of eldritch energy working their way through the Pacific Northwest. Once the time-lapse kicked in and played over the main regional map screen, they'd have a better idea of what they were dealing with.

A week ago, Velasquez and Park, with the help of Roland and a wizard from Seattle, had tracked down the phantasmal entity who had once been a young witch named Caldoria McCluskey. Wraiths in the Other had transformed her into an eldritch crone, a variety of magical lich or vampire-like creature who'd been preying on the magical auras and life force of various casters in Portland since that time.

They'd destroyed what remained of her physical body and captured her life force and arcane essence, only to discover that the witch had been sending her essence off into the void for the probable purpose of infecting other casters and transforming them into an army of the goddamned undead.

Park snorted as they watched the time-lapse. "What the hell does this mean?"

Velasquez didn't know yet. They had some decent ideas, but nothing was certain.

The main map screen depicted the Pacific Northwest region of North America, mainly the states of Washington and Oregon, with a bit of British Columbia, Idaho, California, and Nevada along the edges. Red dots appeared in great profusion in Seattle and worked their way down into Oregon, congregating around Portland and growing into a giant mass that moved slightly southeast and then spread in all directions before vanishing.

The process repeated; the time-lapse was showing a later period, but the pattern was nearly identical.

"Okay," Park began, "so we know Callie deliberately tossed pieces of her, uh, arcane essence off to other places to create more of those things, right? She stole magical energy from random witches, filtered it through her so that it copied her or something, and then sent them on their merry way. But what exactly are those dots, and why do they keep disappearing?"

Velasquez scratched his chin as he thought. Park was sharp, and he was already shaping up to be a good agent, but he hadn't seen some of the shit Velasquez had, let alone the old farts. The universe was a bigger and scarier place than most people knew.

"What if," the senior agent mused, "she isn't infecting people yet, but instead was creating ghost-clones of herself? Not fully developed, but, like, seeds that contained her essence. Like those things in Harry Potter that begin with an 'H' that the bad guy had, sorta."

"Horcruxes," Park chimed in.

"Yeah, thanks. I'm thinking the dots are those prototype clones, heading out to feed on even more witches, then make more copies of themselves at an exponential rate, potentially creating a nearly unlimited army of crones. The vanishing act is them leaving our plane of existence and heading off into the Other."

Park cracked his knuckles. "I've heard about the Other, which means I know you were there, along with those other guys in the crack team."

Velasquez nodded. "Briefly, but the place is real, and it's nothing to fuck around with. But we need to chase these things down, no matter where they go."

They stood up in unison, not hurried but with steady purpose.

"Getting out there," Park added, "and simply observing the things will grant us a better idea of what the fuck they're doing, if nothing else. At this point, it's pure conjecture. No offense."

"None taken," Velasquez replied in a monotone. "We have no experts on eldritch crones, only data files taken from much older cases and vague foreign reports."

Exiting the room within Regional HQ, they headed toward the armory to gear up for a field mission.

CHAPTER TWO

Bailey floated through the air, keeping close to the trees, the better to stay inconspicuous. She could have walked or driven her black Toyota Tundra back home, but it would have taken longer. After the upsetting conversation with Loki, all she wanted was to get back to her bed as quickly as possible. Tomorrow she could fly back up and retrieve the truck.

She passed below the tree line. It was halfway through the magic hour, and the land was growing dark where the pines shadowed it from what little remained of the sun. Familiar slopes and peaks rolled under her, and the summer evening wind felt unusually cool as it rushed by.

She landed on the wooded slope right before her backyard started. The lights were on in her house, and standing by the pole barn that dominated the rear portion of the backyard was a familiar tall, broad-shouldered figure.

Fenris. He'd been waiting for her.

A tremor of nervous cold began in her spine and rattled its way out to her extremities, but with a deep breath and the intense mental discipline she'd cultivated during her training, she dispelled it. Then she walked toward the silhouette.

Fenris stepped out into the semi-light, his eyes hidden by the hood of the coat he always wore. "Bailey. I need to speak to you. But first, how did the arbitration go?"

"Fine," she replied, hoping her voice sounded natural. She was pretty sure it did, but a veteran god might be more sensitive to subtle changes in a person's manner of speaking than she could conceive. "They argued and postured, mostly to make themselves look cool in front of their friends, then I imposed a decent compromise on them, and they grunted and agreed and went home. We'll see if they keep to it. If not, I might have to kick their asses around a little until they behave."

The were-god smiled, an expression not often seen on his grim, craggy face. "Good."

She stopped next to him, where they were mostly hidden from the house's windows behind the pole barn. "What is it you wanted to talk to me about? No offense, but I could use some food."

He answered her with, "I won't keep you long. Something has been troubling me of late, and I wanted to make you aware of it so you can keep your eyes open and know about it if any problems develop."

She allowed her eyes to narrow in concern and gave a slow nod. "Okay. What is it?"

He laid a hand on her shoulder, and she forced herself not to react. He'd done that many times, a warm, fatherly gesture that she had always welcomed.

"I am beginning to fear," he began, "that much, if not all,

of what has happened recently has not been a coincidence, but instead has been orchestrated."

"Oh?" She raised an eyebrow. "By who? And what-all incidents are you referring to? Lots of shit has happened in the last week or so."

The wolf-father inhaled through his nose and seemed to consider his words before he spoke on. "The difficulties you encountered while trying to ascend to the council," he stated, "along with the seemingly random tribulations at the training grounds in the Other, and the minor squabbles among local packs you've been dealing with. And perhaps even worse and more major things from months past."

It was hard not to squirm. What he was saying reminded her too much of what Loki had told her less than half an hour ago.

"I believe," Fenris went on, "that many, if not all of these problems were part of a plan being executed by the other council gods. Which ones, I am not certain—quite possibly all of them. Freya is the main suspect."

She put her hands on her hips, affecting her usual tough, skeptical, but open manner. "What makes you think that? Freya's been kicked off the council for the time being, anyway, and I haven't seen or heard from her. Which is weird, considering she promised she'd mentor me on how to take her place."

Fenris shook his head, his mouth puckering in sour cynicism. "She may have said that she'd help you, but she's still angry and bitter about being dethroned. It's possible she's plotting something. Still, removing her from her position was a step in the right direction. She lacks the direct power she previously had, and she'll need time to recover from how badly you drained her."

The girl admitted that what Fenris was saying made sense. Freya's dislike and distrust of Bailey had long been obvious, and it wasn't inconceivable that she could have been pulling the strings all along.

Had she secretly been working with Aradia and the Venatori, maybe? That might explain how Aradia popped out of nowhere when we started to kick the Order's collective ass. There's no evidence for that, but—

Fenris cut off her ruminations with the next thing he said.

"If only," he sighed, "there were others like you, others of your caliber, who could replace them all."

Her jaw nearly dropped, and had it not been for all the self-discipline she'd cultivated, much of it under Fenris's tutelage, she would not have been able to disguise her shock.

He admitted that he has...ambitions. Designs to take over the council, and that I'm a part of that.

"Yes," the wolf-god went on, "I would not place your full trust in any of them. I'll talk no more about divine politics since much of those are personal matters between us that go back far, far before your birth. I *will* warn you to be vigilant. Keep an eye out for anything suspicious or unusual. Some, if not all, of the deities who sat in judgment before you might be lurking in wait for the opportunity to pounce and neutralize the threat you represent, regardless of whatever ceremony they performed to make you feel at home among them."

As he talked, Bailey's mind went into overdrive. Loki

had primed it to do so. Things began falling into place, and she didn't like the shape they were forming.

Everything had happened so perfectly. Every single event that had *needed* to transpire in order for Bailey to ascend to godhood at Fenris's side *had* done so.

And why, she wondered, would he be so generous and charitable as to give another being so many opportunities to grow in power and influence? Why would he, with his intricate relationships and resentments with the other deities, raise a mortal to the level of a goddess?

He had to have a purpose for her. It made no sense otherwise.

And who better than a dumb, desperate girl like me, who would have done anything to gain the power she needed to get out of that godawful marriage tradition Weres still impose on their kids. If he'd asked me to swim across the Pacific with weights tied to my legs, I'd probably have done it if it meant I didn't have to get married to someone like Dan-fucking-Oberlin.

"Freya," Fenris went on, "lacks power now, but she is still angry. And Loki is a spiteful liar; that is his nature, and it's part of his divine mantle. Coyote is little better than Loki. Thor is not as deceitful as the others, but he's capable of great foolishness. Balder may seem innocent, but he and Freya are very close, so consider that. Thoth may come across as wise and trustworthy, but he is blinded by his adherence to hollow traditions."

Bailey nodded, continuing to make a show of carefully considering her mentor's monologue.

But, she thought, if Loki has it out for me, he could have voted against me during the trials, or come up with an elaborate scheme to screw me over. He's a genius trick-ster. Instead, he came onto my turf to give me a private warning.

"Okay," said Bailey, "I guess I personally haven't seen too much wrongdoing from them, but I'll keep all that in mind. I'm used to being careful. Let me know if you need me for anything, and take care of yourself, too."

She prepared to walk into her house, but Fenris stopped her. "Before you go, give me one quick demonstra-tion of your newly acclimated power. A brief, friendly duel of the sort we used to engage in for practice. For old time's sake."

The faint hint of warmth was back in his gentle smile, and Bailey was confused. Why was she doubting his motives? He'd never done anything but help her.

"Sure, but let's make it fast. I'm hungry."

The tall shaman extended his hands, and they glowed an intense deep purple for a fraction of a second.

It was enough warning for Bailey to conjure an arcane shield of translucent light in front of her with a rippled structure that deflected the powerful bolt that surged from Fenris's hands.

He caught the bolt and threw it back at her. She created an illusory double of herself, covered it with a second shield, and allowed it to deflect the bolt again while she dashed in on the wolf-god's flank and swung a sword-like beam of red plasma at him.

Fenris spun, an indigo blade rising from his fist to meet hers in a shower of sparks while his off hand caught the initial bolt and crushed it into a small glowing coal.

"Good," he stated, stepping back and relaxing. He

dismissed the enchantments in each hand, and Bailey did likewise.

"You are growing in power and ability so fast," he told her. "You completed your education in deflective shields on your own after I walked you through the basic underlying philosophy. Phenomenal. You will soon be the equal of any god, including me."

Raising a hand, he trudged off into the woods beyond the yard, vanishing into the blackness.

The girl stood there, neither moving nor speaking.

Equal to him.

It was past dark, and the werewitch felt foolish for taking her Camaro for the short drive into town, but she'd left the truck up in the mountains, and fetching it would take too long.

She needed to speak to Gunney *now*.

She turned onto the side street off the main road, and her car ascended the gentle slope. She found the auto shop mostly dark, save for a single light in the repair bay closest to the office. As usual, Gunney was hanging out and doing extra work for fun, well past formal closing time. The man loved what he did.

Bailey parked in front, stepped out, and strode toward the bay. She had no doubt that he saw and heard her, but her visits were routine enough that he'd probably wait until she was inside to bother saying hello.

She stepped over the threshold of the open door into the shop. "Hi, Gunney," she called.

The mechanic came around a corner, wiping his face with a grease-smudged rag. "Evening, Bailey. Heard you went off to play referee to some bucks who had a hunting dispute or some shit like that."

"Yep," she replied, eyeing him.

Gunney was short and thick-bodied, though not overweight, with a full beard and shaggy hair that he usually hid beneath an old, battered baseball cap. The skin around his eyes crinkled when he smiled. He'd raised Bailey as much as her own father had.

"What's up?" she asked.

He gestured at the car in front of him. "This thing, that's what."

She nodded and looked it over. It was a '96 Chevy Caprice in simple white with steel rims. Okay-enough car, but nothing special. Nothing appeared obviously wrong with it, so she guessed it was here for routine maintenance.

"Sometimes," Gunney murmured, his voice growing softer and more distant as he gazed at the vehicle, "the easy, straightforward stuff can clear the mind. Might seem boring, but I honestly enjoy stuff like this in between the tougher jobs and the more esoteric rides we get. So," he turned to catch her eyes, his own twinkling, "you being a goddess and all, are you too big in the britches now to help an old man turn a wrench?"

She laughed. "You know damn well that's a stupid question. It's physically impossible for me to get too big to work on cars."

"Oh, right," he snarked. "I keep forgetting you technically work here since I don't see you around much."

She pouted. "Sorry, old man. You know how it goes.

Cosmic duties and shit…"

They fell into an easy, comfortable silence as the tasks before them progressed. Moving at a steady but unhurried pace, they performed a basic oil change, then installed new pads on the front brakes, topped off the brake and wiper fluid, and checked the spark plugs, replacing the ones that were getting worn.

Midway into the process, Gunney asked, "So, what's on your mind? You seem busy these days, so I kinda doubt you're here out of sheer boredom."

"A whole bunch of disturbing crap," she muttered. "But you know, I'm hungry as a dog. Somehow I forgot to eat after I got back from playing mediator for those two packs up the mountain."

Gunney nodded. "That can be remedied, especially since I could use a dinner break myself."

He went to the fridge and returned with two subs he'd purchased from the local sandwich shop earlier, leaving them in the fridge to stay nice and cold.

"Kinda figured you'd be around," he shrugged. "Dunno why. Something in the air changes when I suspect you'll show up, maybe. Oh, wait." He went back to the refrigerator again and came back with a couple glass bottles of Mexican Coke. "I know orange is your usual favorite, but we don't get this stuff often."

She nodded. "That'll do." They washed their hands, ate, and drank.

Partway into the meal, Bailey told the mechanic about Loki's appearance and all he'd said, and how she'd met Fenris right afterward and been unable to avoid teasing new meanings out of things he said.

"I'm not sure," she confessed. "I don't know what to believe. Fenris is...my friend, but I wonder now. I can't help it."

Gunney shook his head. "Shit on a shingle. Every time you get a concern, you come to me with something so crazy it makes the insanity from before look kinda reasonable. Well, if I see Fenris, I won't say anything about any of this. First time I met him, he seemed...shady, at first, and yet, like you've said, he's never really *done* anything but help us and be good to us. I don't know, either."

Her shoulders slumped. She'd hoped the mechanic would be able to give her a clearer answer.

"Well," he continued, "I will say that it's always best to worry about problems closer to home first. If bigger stuff comes down the pipe, we'll deal with it like we always have. Start with the simple stuff."

Bailey finished eating and crumpled the sandwich wrapper to toss into a nearby trash can.

Gunney gestured behind him. "For example, the remaining simple stuff that that thing needs done, such as rotating the tires. Me, I'm old and crotchety, my back's going bad, and you'll have to hear me bitching and moaning the whole time. Whereas, a young kid like you with wolf-shifter strength and divine powers should be able to make short work of it."

Laughing, she stood up and completed the job while he watched. It was good to know exactly what she was supposed to do for once.

One of the younger agents, greener than Park, looked at Velasquez. "This shit's real, isn't it, sir?"

"Affirmative, Norman," the senior agent replied. "You'll see how real in a minute."

Velasquez was the acting team leader for the current force, which numbered a dozen men including him, Park, and Norman. They had congregated in the sub-basement of the Agency's HQ after suiting up.

All twelve wore silver-chrome breastplates and helmets over standard paramilitary body armor. They all carried weapons that resembled compact short-barreled rifles, the same bright hue as the armor, paired with wrist-mounted storage tanks. At their sides, they wore the Agency's new anti-magic combat knives.

Velasquez faced the others. "Everyone ready?"

"Yes, sir," they replied in unison.

The team leader turned back to the device they'd set up. It had an expandable circular center and four pins attached to cords which they'd anchored to the four corners of the far wall. Counterintuitively, that had caused the central circle to stretch into a vertical oval the size of a narrow doorway.

Agent Park flipped a switch on a small remote, and the thing on the wall charged. Deep violet and bright magenta light filtered down the cords and swirled in the oval portion, which was specially calibrated arcanoplasm the Agency had harnessed for use in opening portals to other domains.

No one had tested it. This would be the Agency's first foray into the Other under their own power. When Velasquez and his men had gone through before to aid in the fight against the goddess Aradia, they'd relied upon the abilities of supernatural casters to open the gate.

Velasquez stepped forward and put his hand on a dial on the side of the oval doorway. It was a key of sorts; the Agency had mapped enough of the Other to be able to track specific types of emanations. Referencing the tracking device in his other hand, he set the coordinates for the spot that was currently showing the largest amount of activity related to their recent monitoring of the eldritch crones.

The light grew brighter, then the swirling radiance within the oval gateway attained depth. It was no longer a flat object but a passage.

The team leader took a deep breath. "Maintain formation. After me."

He stepped into the portal, hoping the boys in the lab hadn't flubbed the technology. He was a brave man, but he had no desire to end up between dimensions or accidentally fall into a steaming pot of soup resting on Satan's table in Hell. That would be *bad*.

Freezing cold swept through him, and there was a sense of dizziness and disorientation, then Velasquez's foot connected with solid rock. He took three steps, then another, shook his head to clear it, and came to a halt. He could hear other agents streaming out of the doorway behind him.

They had emerged into the desolate wasteland to end all desolate wastelands. It was like the surface of the moon, though the barren rock that stretched for untold leagues before them was a concentrated red, whereas the sky was an angry bruise-purple.

Behind them was a flat plateau. In front of them lay a cliff's edge, which opened onto a broad, deep canyon. Something was moving in the half-shadowed depths below.

"Well," Park's voice commented, "that was a hell of a rush. Only lasted a second, though. Christ, this place is like the Halloween version of northern Arizona, but I don't think the canyon is quite as big."

"Quiet," Velasquez replied, though the air had a flat, dead quality which muffled the sounds around them. It made no sense since the open nature of the landscape meant any noise ought to travel for miles and echo for entire minutes.

The Other was not bound to the same laws of nature as the Earth.

At the team leader's gesture of command, the dozen men moved forward, their boots making the softest of thuds on the lifeless stone as they advanced toward the precipice. The full vista of the dark red canyon below opened before them.

The gorge was impressive. Just as striking as the striated layers of rock plunging hundreds of yards below them was the shifting, squirming mass that filled it, the chaos of uncountable forms, all of them identical, milling around within a confined space.

Velazquez felt as though his stomach were sinking between his knees. "Shit," he muttered as he checked the tracking device. It was beeping frantically, and the display screen had brought up so many red dots that it looked like a solid wall of scarlet.

The canyon was brimming with duplicates of Callie

McCluskey in her loathsome semi-corporeal form as an eldritch crone. Ragged, translucent, hag-like forms were everywhere. Their estimate that she was creating a legion of clones had not been an overstatement. Velasquez guessed there was a minimum of three hundred down there, more like five.

Norman came up beside the team leader and gawked stupidly at the nightmare vision. "We're fighting those things?"

Velasquez puffed himself up. "Not right this minute," he stated, "but yes. We have the technology to eliminate them, but as you may have surmised, there are more than we expected. Attacking them now would be a gross error."

"I agree," said Park. "This *isn't* Sparta. But we have to do something."

"Of course," the senior agent agreed. "If these things aren't stopped and soon, they'll launch their assault and overrun the entire northwest coast of America, possibly more. Averting stuff like that, gentlemen, is why our organization exists."

He bade them retreat, and everyone filed back through the portal, reemerging in the mundane basement chamber. Velasquez shut off the gateway device as soon as everyone was accounted for.

He turned to his men. "Don't get too comfortable. We will be moving soon, but we're going to need help to take on that many of the fuckers."

Nods of agreement went around the group. Even the boldest of them was ashen-faced.

"Fortunately," Velasquez added, pulling out his cell phone, "I just happen to have a goddess on speed dial."

CHAPTER THREE

Given the nature of the discussion that was about to take place, Bailey sat at the head of the dinner table. It felt weird and borderline blasphemous. Normally the space was reserved for her father. He wasn't home much since his various odd jobs and social calls took him all over the Hearth Valley, and sometimes into the mountains or hollows beyond. He often stayed where he was working for weeks or months at a time, but she still thought of it as his permanent place.

Nonetheless, this was a serious council.

Roland, the slender blond wizard from Seattle and her husband-to-be, sat at her right hand, and Jacob, the tall and square-jawed eldest of her brothers, at her left. Beyond them sat her two youngest brothers, Kurt and Russell. Kurt was of a height with Jacob though scrawnier, and Russell was taller, darker, and heavier than either.

In the middle of the table rested the remains of the pot roast they'd devoured for dinner. Empty glasses had been pushed to the opposite end from Bailey.

"Okay," she began, "this is...not easy for me to talk about. Not in the slightest. But you guys are my trusted inner circle, and I need you to do two things for me. First is to listen and consider that this might be something major. Second is not to jump to conclusions too soon. I myself am still not *certain*. Do you understand?"

They all did. In their eyes, she saw concern, trepidation, and burning curiosity.

She opened up and told them everything. At first the words came out slowly and hesitantly; she was uncomfortable discussing the topic. Then the blockage passed, and the words spilled out in a quickening flood as the emotions behind them grew stronger.

When she mentioned Loki's visit and all that he'd apprised her of, Roland seemed keen to offer his own commentary, but seeing that she needed to get it all out at once, he held back, waiting until she was finished.

She went on to describe her meeting with Fenris behind the house the previous night and spoke of the terrible thoughts that had filled her mind as everything he said took on a seemingly sinister new meaning in light of Loki's report.

She concluded by reminding them that there was no way to be one hundred percent sure. Not yet.

"Roland," she said, "I remember that you always were, well, standoffish with Fenris, even when I trusted him completely. Maybe you were right after all, but please do this for me. Don't jump at the opportunity to get back at him or anything like that, because if Loki's the one who's lying, I'll never forgive myself if we turn against Fenris for no reason. He's...he's done so much for me."

The wizard nodded. "If what Loki says is true, Fenris has done it mostly for *himself*. However, as I wanted to say earlier, Loki is not the most trustworthy character in the old Norse legends. His suspicions line up a little too neatly for us *not* to consider what he said, but it's possible that this is a masterstroke of misdirection on his part."

"Yeah," Bailey acceded, "that occurred to me. Which is why I'd say it's important for us to be on guard and prepared, but also to keep playing along like everything is normal until we can find out more."

Russell grunted. "Agreed."

Kurt shook his head. "This crap is mind-boggling, but yeah, agreed."

Jacob remained silent, his brow furrowed. Bailey asked him what he thought.

"I," he began, then paused. "I just…Fenris is *our god*. He's the father of werewolves. His whole reason for existence is to watch out for us. That's the way it works, isn't it?"

Bailey closed her eyes, feeling another stab of pain at the implications. "That's how it's supposed to be, yes, but it's possible that everything will be changing for all of us soon."

Roland put his hand atop hers, and she looked at him.

"Roland, I'd like you to get in touch with your friend—Dante, I think his name is. And anyone else you know from the caster community around here. We want to make sure that the witches are mostly still on my side and ready to act if we need them. I'm a goddess of your people as well as my own, but it's better if they want to help."

He ran a hand through his hair. "Understood. I have contacts, and most witches hold me in pretty high esteem these days. If we can demonstrate that there's a legitimate threat brewing, I'd say we can count on a significant number of them."

"Okay, great. Jacob, and Kurt and Russell," she went on. "You guys need to be my contacts among Weres. Talk to everyone around here, including anyone who knows wolves in other nearby areas, and maybe some of those people we helped awhile back from other parts of the country, too. Again, I'm not issuing goddess-orders. I only want to get an idea about if they'll back us up if worse comes to worst."

Jacob still brooded, so the two younger brothers spoke for the male Nordins.

"Shouldn't be hard," Kurt quipped. "Most of those guys kinda pledged loyalty to you months ago anyway, and you're technically their goddess now, too."

Russell said darkly, "We'll do whatever we have to."

Jacob finally nodded, though he looked dazed and unhappy.

As a sense of purpose settled in among them, Bailey spread her hands and concluded, "I truly don't know what to expect, but there's major trouble brewing, that's for damn sure. Since if Fenris is innocent, that means that Loki is trying to turn us against him, and that's equally bad. If we need an army, it's better to have one on standby rather than try to assemble one out of thin air."

Roland stood up. "I'll call Dante as soon as we're done here. *Man*, a possible betrayal between the gods and a battle amidst the pantheon. Come what may, at least it's going to be *interesting*."

Kurt remarked, "That's not the term I'd use, but it'll do."

Bailey sensed rather than saw that she had a visitor. Sitting up in bed, rubbing her eyes, and glancing at the clock, she saw that it was 3:02 a.m. Beside her, Roland lay in a deep sleep, snoring gently. She did not wake him up.

She climbed off the mattress and went to the window barefoot, looking out between the blinds. Standing on her lawn was a tall, hooded, broad-shouldered figure. He beckoned for her to come to him.

She stared down, then let the blinds fall closed and almost stumbled back into bed.

Go talk to him, she told herself. Every time he shows up, you've paid attention because it's always something important.

The werewitch padded out of her room and down the stairs, taking care not to make any noise that would rouse her brothers. Gently, she opened the back door and eased out onto the damp grass.

Fenris turned to her, and they met halfway across the lawn.

"Thank you for coming out," he began. "I didn't want to disturb your family while they rest, but I must speak to you. Walk with me to the edge of the woods."

She hated that it scared her to hear him say that. Absolutely hated it. Fenris was her teacher and friend, and he had never harmed her in any way.

"Sure," she said and followed the wolf-god as he strode toward the north side of the yard, leaving the Nordin property and beginning to ascend the semi-wooded slope. They moved without talking, and there was a heavy, glum quality to the silence between them that bothered her.

Finally, Fenris spoke.

"This is difficult to discuss," he began, and Bailey's heart skipped a beat, "but one of your duties as a goddess is upon you. You knew that things like this could happen, of course. Dangers might emerge from places you'd never heard of; things most mortals have never heard of that can destroy them all the same."

The girl inhaled and did not respond right away. Though what Fenris described sounded serious, he did not seem to be talking about anything pertaining to Loki's efforts to inform against him.

Or to what Bailey had told her family and friends.

"What is it?" she asked. "Is it something we have to deal with right away?"

He stopped and turned to her, as they'd just now entered the forest. "I'm afraid so. There is another plane of existence being threatened by an influx of frost trolls. Perhaps you'd think that this was none of your business, but in fact, it means that Earth will be threatened if something isn't done."

"Frost trolls?" she sputtered.

"Not the frost *giants* from the legends of our pantheon," Fenris clarified, "but bad enough. For various reasons, the barriers between realms have recently weakened, and dangerous creatures like them have been unleashed. The more peaceful and civilized peoples of the universes are threatened by incursions from creatures of their ilk, and when they've finished with their current target, they will move on to our world. We have a responsibility to stop them."

The girl had not expected anything remotely like this. She felt as though she'd missed an important day of class right before a test. "How?" she inquired.

"By cutting them off at their source," the wolf-father stated.

All of a sudden, Bailey found herself wishing for a nice cup of Russell's coffee. "The source, meaning their homeworld?"

"Yes." Fenris's manner was growing distant, so he was probably getting ready to open a portal and plan his strategy of attack and defense. "They are dangerous, but by no means invincible. The two of us can deal with a great many of them."

I don't doubt it, Bailey thought. *But if these trolls are such a big threat, then shouldn't we be asking for reinforcements?*

The wolf-god went on, "They are large—noticeably bigger than humans—and physically imposing and strong. They also resist magic. They're not immune, but you will find that it takes more than usual to defeat them, so it will be like trying to channel in the Other before you learned to circumvent that domain's limitations. Though frost trolls are tough, they're not very intelligent, and their usual battle strategy is to act as juggernauts in a frontal assault. That is nothing to scoff at, so be ready."

Sighing, the girl resigned herself to whatever was to come. Despite her suspicions, she had no concrete evidence that Fenris was acting on malevolent or dishonest motives.

He spread his hands while chanting, and a wavering

doorway that looked like glowing amethyst liquid appeared in front of him.

"This," he added, "will be an all-out, no-holds-barred fight. We will be struggling for our lives and those of our families and friends. Treating it as anything less risks leaving our realms open to the trolls' onslaught."

"Okay," Bailey agreed. "But do me one favor. You first." She motioned at the portal.

He looked at her for a split second, then said, "Very well," and stepped through. Exhaling, the girl followed him. She hoped she was doing the right thing.

Agent Velasquez paused at the edge of the little town. Park, who was in excellent shape and tended to move fast, got three steps ahead of him before he noticed that his partner had fallen behind. He turned around.

"What's the matter?" Park asked.

Velasquez pulled out his phone to double-check for messages or missed calls. Nothing.

"If Bailey isn't answering us, it probably means she's not currently located in the same plane of existence as we are. That poses certain problems, especially since last time I was here, the townsfolk had only the vaguest idea of where she might be or how the hell to get hold of her."

Park shrugged. "Someone would have seen or heard something. There's nothing else we can do, besides."

"True enough," Velasquez conceded. "We'll start with the mechanic since he's closer."

They left their car at the sheriff's station. Sheriff

Browne didn't know the girl's whereabouts either, and he seemed hesitant to get too involved with whatever shenanigans a pair of federal agents might be here pursuing. A short walk through the community would turn up more opportunities to talk to people than driving would.

Only a small handful of pedestrians were out and about, though, and most of them gave the pair a wide berth. One woman seemed to recognize Velasquez and said hello, but she hadn't seen Bailey in a while, nor heard anything about where she was.

When they arrived at Gunney's auto shop, the proprietor noticed them approaching and wiped his hands off before coming out to greet them in the front lot.

"Hi," he called. "Velasquez, I remember you, but I haven't met the other gentleman. I'm Gunney."

"Park," the agent replied. "Nice to meet you. As you can imagine, we have some questions."

The mechanic nodded in a sharp motion. "Right. Well, first of all, I haven't seen Bailey since the night before last."

Velasquez adjusted his glasses. "That answers our primary question. Have you heard from her, or do you have any idea where she might be? We've tried to call her several times but have not gotten a response."

Gunny shook his head. "Afraid not. She comes and goes. Last I heard, you guys were aware that she has, uh, certain new responsibilities these days, so if she's not in town, then I'd guess she's off doing *that* kinda stuff."

As the agents frowned, the older man flipped his cap off his head, allowing his shaggy hair to breathe in the heat before pulling back on. "Might want to check with her brothers. The previous guy, Townsend, knew where they lived, so I'd be shocked if you gentlemen don't have access to that information."

"Yes," said Velasquez. "We'll check it out. Thanks for cooperating."

"No problem." The mechanic waved to them as he turned back toward his shop. "If you'll excuse me, I got some grease to monkey. Good luck."

The agents strode back to their car at a fast clip. Velasquez fired up the engine immediately, while Park brought up the Nordin family's address on his device. "Got it. That was easy."

Velasquez pulled onto Main Street and headed west, then north down a side road. "Of course it was."

The drive took only a few minutes. When they pulled into the front lot of the old farmhouse, the eldest of the brothers, Jacob, emerged to greet them before they could knock.

"Hi," he called. "No offense, but we were kinda hoping things would stay quiet enough that you guys wouldn't come a-calling again."

"Yeah," Velasquez remarked, "same."

Park snorted. "Speak for yourself. I was bored as fuck."

Jacob let them in and offered them drinks, which they declined. The younger siblings, Russell and Kurt, drifted over to watch as the two men stood in the small foyer area.

"Okay," Velasquez began, "I won't waste your time. Where's Bailey? We need her help."

Russell and Kurt grimaced as Jacob stepped closer. "Unfortunately, we were wondering the same thing. She disappeared last night. Based on her scent and some minor tracks, she got out of bed and walked out back sometime late at night or early in the morning. We lost the trail right at the edge of the woods out there." He gestured with his chin in the appropriate direction. "My guess is that she went off on a divine errand or something, possibly with you-know-who. Marcus. You met him, right?"

Park snapped his fingers. "You mean Fenris. I read the file, and Velasquez was right there with him during the Aradia incident."

"Fine," Jacob responded. "Anyway, we haven't heard from her, but we're hoping *someone* has. Any minute, we're expecting—"

Someone knocked on the door. Russell sprang up to answer it, and when he swung open the door, two slender blond men in their twenties stood side by side on the porch.

"—them," the eldest brother finished. "We were expecting them."

Roland waved. "Hi, everyone, including you guys." He looked at the agents. "What terrible thing is happening now that you had no choice but to pay us a visit?"

Dante frowned. "Actually, I was hoping to see you two again. Were you able to dissipate the energy from that ghost-thing we captured?"

Velasquez let out a half-sigh, half-groan. "You'd better come in and sit down."

The wizards did, accepting cups of coffee from the Nordin brothers and waiting for the inevitable bombshell, whatever it was.

"First," Park inquired, "what were you guys off doing? You're not in trouble, but we'd like to have an idea of what's going on."

Roland explained that Bailey had asked him to link up with Dante again and speak to the Northwestern witch community in case they needed backup if anything strange happened. Since she wasn't here when he woke up, which was not unusual, he'd gone about his business. He did not offer any further details. Dante, sensing that it would be best to only reveal the full truth if they were pressed, kept his mouth shut as well.

At the end of their account, Velasquez smoothed his hair and scowled. "I see. You have piqued our curiosity, but we've got bigger fish to fry. We could use Bailey's help, and yours."

The dark-suited pair told the wizards about all that had happened concerning Callie and the army of eldritch crones she'd created. Roland and Dante went increasingly pale as the agents' story progressed.

"So," Velasquez concluded, "in saving the whole region from this fuckery, we stand a much better chance with skilled casters such as you on our side. You temporarily defeated her before, after all. You can defend against these things' attacks and help disperse their magical energies while we mop them up with our new weapons and tools. It isn't going to be easy or simple, no matter what."

Roland pinched his nose, but it was Dante who said, "Oh, of course not. When is it ever?"

"Right," Park concurred. "We don't have the numbers or firepower to challenge the whole horde at once, so we'll need to make repeated incursions against portions of it, wiping out swaths of Ms. McCluskey's etheric doubles before she can break off even more of the goddamn things after feeding on witch-energy. We'll need to stay on top of things, move fast, hit hard, and cut her off from any route of escape."

"Sounds fun," Roland grumbled. "But the thought of *Callie* taking over all of Washington and Oregon is too horrifying to consider. I heard that before she moved to Seattle, she used to torture her little brother by locking him in the bathroom and making him listen to Nicki Minaj at max volume for an hour or more at a time. We don't want a person like that at the forefront of an undead apocalypse."

Dante nodded. "Yeah, what he said. Can we scout them out first, though? Like, accompany you guys to their hiding place to get a clear idea of what we're dealing with?"

The agents glanced at each other. Velasquez replied, "Yes. We'll need a short time to convene every extra agent we can get for the operation. Let's have a quick discussion of strategy, then we'll need to get moving."

As they discussed their plans, though, Velasquez could not stop wondering how they'd be able to manage without a certain newly-minted deity.

CHAPTER FOUR

"Don't worry," Roland reassured them, "we know how to open portals to the Other. It's no big deal."

Agent Park spread his hands. "Okay, but do you know exactly where we're going? That's where our equipment comes in handy."

The wizard scowled. "I don't, so good point. We'll use you guys' weird magical trampoline or collapsible closet or whatever the hell that is."

Dante squinted at him. *"Collapsible closet?* It looks nothing like that. More like a parachute."

"Quiet," Velasquez snapped as he checked his tracking device and punched in the coordinates.

After comparing notes and agreeing upon a rough strategy for what they'd do during their reconnaissance mission, the four had gone out to the Nordin family's pole barn in the backyard (which doubled as Roland's bedroom) and set up the agents' portable gateway device against the far wall. Roland was dubious as to whether it would actually work, but...

The machine hummed, and purplish light flowed down the cords toward the central oval portion. It lit up, disclosing a surface identical to the portals Roland had opened or seen Fenris and other beings open via traditional magic.

"Well, then," he said, blinking. "The Agency's research and development team is putting our tax dollars to good use, I see."

Dante raised a finger. "That reminds me, what kind of benefits package do you guys get? Like healthcare, retirement, and all that shit."

Velasquez smiled. "The best."

"Figures," the young wizard responded. "When all the scary monsters are dead, will we get our own?"

The agents shrugged, and Park answered, "Uh, that's not our department. Sorry."

The device stabilized and beeped to indicate that the portal was safe to use. Velasquez motioned them to move out but stepped through first. He had, of course, equipped his silver-chrome carbine with its accompanying mounted wrist tank and wore anti-magic body armor. Park was similarly equipped.

The junior agent remained behind to ensure the wizards complied. "Well," Roland pointed out, "the portal *looks* right, anyway." He went through, with Dante right behind him.

They emerged onto a cliff of dark red rock that loomed above a deep, broad gorge or canyon within a vast stony desert. Above, the sky was a dark and menacing purple.

Roland whistled. "Okay, I have to admit, I've never seen this place, and I would not have known how the hell to transport us here. Makes me wonder how big the Other truly is, given all the different parts of it we've been to."

Velasquez held up a hand. "Keep your voice down. Move slowly and carefully to the edge of that cliff and have a look down into the canyon."

The two wizards did as the agent suggested, hunching over and treading softly to avoid making noise. The cliff-side fell away, revealing the huge gorge below, which was crawling with hideous, ragged forms—hundreds of them. Some were nearly transparent, but many had attained full solidity of form.

Roland's jaw dropped as his face fell and his eyes widened. He glanced at Dante and saw the same expression on the other young man's face. They backed up until the cliff blocked them from the sight of anything in the canyon, then turned to face the agents.

"Well," Dante gasped, "this is, you know, *really, really bad.*"

Roland rubbed his right eye. "I concur. We need an army for this, not just a task force or whatever. I'm going to suggest that we pull out right away and rethink our whole strategy."

Park made a grumbling sound, and Velasquez sighed. "Strategizing is exactly what we're trying to do, but yes, let's leave. We have to start gathering the other available agents, and if you guys can get your friends to volunteer, so much the better."

Before they could stride back through the portal, though, dim shapes appeared above the rim of a crevasse right behind the gateway.

"Shit!" Park cursed. The four fell into fighting stances,

then the agents raised their weapons as the casters readied spells.

A dozen of the ghostly witch-creatures streamed toward them, letting out soft yet eerie howls that were half-composed of sonic vibrations. The rest of the sound was a psionic effect. Their rags billowed around them despite the absence of a breeze, and their rotting, translucent arms reached out.

Roland conjured a quartet of shields that enveloped the mortals, leaving small spaces for the agents' guns, while Dante summoned gouts of fire from the ground and shards of ice from the sky to strike at the crones from above and below.

They retaliated with flurries of plasma sparks, miniature earthquakes that threatened to shake the four off their feet, and psychic blasts of concentrated fear.

Roland focused on dealing with the subtle stuff—defense and emotional bolstering—while the other three handled offense. The agents deployed their anti-magic rifles and the bright green beams cut through the witches with ease, dissipating half of them into masses of swirling particles.

The others hesitated, and Roland joined Dante in hitting them with powerful lightning bolts that burned away most of their mass. The crones managed another wave of attacks, which the wizards blocked before the agents cut them down and sucked the remaining arcane matter into their wrist-mounted tanks.

Velasquez motioned toward the portal. "Come on. The others probably noticed all that commotion. We don't need to deal with any more at the moment."

They ran through the portal, stumbling awkwardly into Bailey's pole barn on the other side, panting.

Velasquez turned and shut off the gateway device immediately. The purple light died, leaving the building dim.

The four spent a moment looking at each other. The combat had been brief but intense, and the mere squad they'd faced was nothing compared to the entire horde.

"So," Park remarked, "the boys in R&D said that the new model tanks," he tapped the object attached to his wrist, "will come with a current you can run through it that purges the damn things on the spot without us having to bring them back to HQ, but they haven't distributed them yet."

"Right," Velasquez confirmed. "For now, we'll have to head back to base to deal with it. But we need to go there anyway."

Roland shook his head. "No shit. Like I said, an army. And even then, we're probably going to have to make a bunch of small guerilla raids or harrying strikes to reduce their numbers. We won't have the firepower to steamroll the entire agglomeration of those things."

Park gave him an appreciative nod. "You know a thing or two about tactics. Not bad."

Dante added, "I'll start rallying the witch community. They know what happened before when the original Callie killed people to revive herself, so most of them won't deny the reality of what's happening."

Roland chimed in, "I'll see if I can get the were-shamans to help us, but it would be good to have Bailey around. I don't know what she's dealing with, but this crone army could overrun us before she's halfway done with it."

Velasquez thanked them. "All right, we need to leave. Keep your phones on, and be ready for action. Soon."

The four went their separate ways, their minds were heavy with plans, concerns, determination, and, whether they admitted it or not, gut-wrenching fear.

***

Bailey stepped out of the dizzying cold of the gateway into a realm that was equally cold but clear and bright. She paused to catch her breath, the chill of the air making her breath rasp in her throat as she inhaled. Fenris closed the portal.

"We are here," he said. "This mountain pass lies at the edge of the frost trolls' realm. Beyond it, behind us, is the path that leads to Asgard, where my family dwells."

The girl looked around. The pass was at least half a mile wide, and steep cliffs of sheer stone rose to either side before rambling off into long lines of peaks in either direction. Ahead of them was a vast snowy plain dotted with evergreen trees, which thickened to a Nordic-style forest farther out.

Snow fell from the sky, not as in a blizzard, but as a gentle shower of thick, soft, white flakes. The sky, oddly enough, was bright blue and cloudless. There was no visible sun but plenty of light. The scene reminded Bailey of an idealized winter day as depicted in a Christmas painting or a photograph of a skiing vacation.

She glanced over her shoulder. The pass rose and narrowed behind them, trailing off into a mass of white-golden light as it neared the home of the Norse gods.

"Wait," she commented. "Asgard? I thought you said we were here to protect Earth?"

"Yes," replied the wolf-father. "Both. If the trolls break through in sufficient numbers and are able to invade Asgard, they will have access to your realm via the hub of gateways within mine. We cannot allow that."

She nodded. It made sense, but on some level, she wondered if she was being talked into doing the deities' dirty work rather than defending her home and people.

Before she could ponder how this might fit in with Loki's accusations, something happened.

The ground began to shake. Subtly at first, but then the effect became stronger and more noticeable. It was accompanied by a shuffling rumble: the sound of many huge and heavy feet running through snow.

"Be ready," Fenris urged. "We don't know how many of them there will be, or what they might throw at us. Remember, they fight via direct assault and brute force, relying upon their size and resistance to magic."

The werewitch steeled herself. She assumed that her mentor referred to magically-conjured attacks, but she wondered if they would be able to resist parts of their domain being used against them via telekinesis?

They were about to find out.

Trolls, three dozen or more, burst out of the tree line of the forest and onto the plain, kicking up snow in alabaster showers that glinted in the bright light. They roared like bears, and they looked more similar to bears than to any other creature Bailey knew of, though the resemblance was not perfect. They were humanoid and had tusks protruding from their lower jaws like those of boars.

Many wielded clubs that were little more than small uprooted trees. Others had crude axes or spears with stone heads. A few, probably commanders or chieftains or champions, had primitive rough-forged weapons of iron, mainly swords or hammers. Most wore armor of bone, tree bark, or shoddy leather.

Fenris barked, "Get them!" and bolted toward the advancing horde. There were now another two dozen behind the first wave, and possibly more still hidden by the trees.

Bailey didn't hesitate. She forgot her suspicions of her teacher once combat was upon them; nothing welded a bond between sentient beings faster than the camaraderie of shared danger. She charged.

Ten yards ahead of her, Fenris roared and transformed. His coat fell away in tatters as he shifted into a wolf-like monstrosity as tall as a two-story house. She'd seen him in this form only once before when he'd revealed his true identity to her and a rebellious group of the Eastmoor Pack's young bucks.

Then the first of the trolls crashed into him and came within blasting distance of Bailey, and there was no more time for memories. Only battle.

The girl sent a sonic-concussive shockwave across the ground, kicking up thick sheets of snow to obscure the trolls' vision. That halted or slowed most of the front line, and she followed it up with a forked bolt of lightning that drew extra conductivity from the melted snow and the trolls reeled, hurt but not dead. She'd hoped it would have done more damage, but Fenris had warned her that the creatures resisted magic.

The wolf-father had stomped down on two of them and taken a third in his enormous jaws, whipping it around before biting it in half. The bloody pieces fell to the whitened ground as more of the beasts swarmed him, hooting and swinging their primitive weapons.

Bailey turned to face the first of those who'd gotten past her magical assault. She conjured a long plasma blade from her fist and smashed it into them, knowing she'd have to rely on her strength as a lycanthrope as much if not more than her magic as a werewitch and a goddess.

But she was a fighter long before she could cast spells. Her crackling arcane blade pierced the throat and skull of the first troll, dropping it where it stood, then everything became chaos around her.

The last of the trolls fell dead, the impact of its heavy body kicking up clouds of pinkish-red snow around it. With its collapse, silence set in across the plain.

Fenris watched as Bailey stood and glanced around, her eyes wide and lungs heaving. It took her a moment to realize the battle was over. They'd destroyed the first wave.

"We did it," she said. "Damn."

He, back in humanoid form and having reconjured his

coat around him, put a hand on her shoulder. "We did. But there will be more, and soon. Perhaps in an hour, perhaps a day. Rest now. I will make a fire and hunt meat to sustain us. Wait here."

The two of them quickly gathered wood fragments from splintered trees and broken weapons, then used them to ignite a good-sized blaze. Bailey huddled next to it, the cold of the realm getting to her since her blood no longer pumped with the exertion of combat.

Fenris supposed she knew that, as a goddess, she could easily regulate her body temperature, but her human side seemed to prefer the traditional comforts of a fire and a heavy coat or blanket. He left her there to rest as he bounded off into the forest.

Soon enough, he found an elk the size of a large human vehicle like an SUV and pounced on it in his wolf form. His powerful jaws crushed its neck before it could flee. It was a simple matter to gut and clean the carcass and drag it back to the campfire.

Bailey looked up at him with an eager expression. "Nice," she quipped. "Not sure I ever had elk before. That one's massive, but I'm hungry enough to eat half of it."

They set chunks of meat to roast on a big spit. Fenris tore some of the meat off the carcass to eat while it was still mostly raw, as he preferred. Bailey made no criticism.

"Bailey," he began, "it will take a while to cook meat, and someone needs to remain on guard here. I want you to stay by this fire while I scout ahead to learn how many more of the trolls are nearby and what their next movements might be."

She frowned. "That sounds dangerous. For both of us, I mean."

"Perhaps," he conceded, "but there is no other way since we don't have reliable allies we can call upon. And since I know this place, I can return to your side instantly if I must."

Still the girl grimaced, though Fenris could not be certain if it was out of concern, or...something else.

He left her by the cookfire, shifted again into his giant lupine form, and bounded across the plain and through the woods, clearing huge distances at tremendous speed. In moments, Bailey was far out of sight or earshot.

The frost trolls were easy to smell. Near the far end of the forest, he sensed a large gathering of them, as he'd expected. His massive furry body plunged ahead, and his senses were sharp enough that he easily avoided crashing into any of the trees.

He came to the edge of a clearing filled with stumps, icy rocks, and burnt-out shells of pines. The space was elbow to elbow with trolls, which amounted to only fifty or sixty, given how much room they each took up. They did not notice him.

At the center of the throng was a raised mound of earth on which rested a great chair or throne carved from solid ice. In it sat the largest and yet most human-like of all the trolls, and on his head, he wore a crown of sharpened stone and bones held together by a ring of ice. He rested a huge warhammer made of the same materials, though reinforced with iron, on his shoulder.

It was the king of the frost trolls who first noticed Fenris.

He gave a snorting grunt. "What are you doing here?" he rasped in his guttural language. Most of his hair was white, but he had a long, dark beard in which icicles had formed.

As he spoke, the other trolls turned around and faced the wolf-god, who'd shifted back into the shape of a tall, hooded man.

"Good day," Fenris greeted them. "You know me already. I've spoken to you, but not as Fenris. It was I, in the guise of the creature you called Skarlang, who prompted you to attack the borders of Asgard. I am your ally and confidant."

Rumbles of surprise or apprehension went around the creatures. The king waved for them to be silent.

He asked, "How do we know you speak the truth?

Fenris shifted into the likeness of Skarlang, an entity he had invented who would look like an abused and pitiful frost troll, supposedly taken as a slave by the gods, so as to gain the trolls' sympathy. Then he shifted back.

The creatures started chattering again, suitably impressed. They were not smart enough to consider that some other being might have aped the same disguise, though that was not the case. Fenris had been Skarlang all along.

The wolf-father spread his arms. "You see," he proclaimed, "the time has come to start Ragnarök. The gods are weak and confused, and the legitimacy of their reign is much disputed. We must attack them, weaken them, and finally overthrow them. Such is my goal."

Confused and excited growls came from the crowd, and heavy brows furrowed.

"But," Fenris added, "you, and other peoples who have been left in the dust by the lords of Asgard, are to rise up under your own banners, not mine. I do not mean to take command of your people, nor rule instead of your king. I seek only to give us a common goal on which to focus."

The king demanded, "What goal, Fenris-Skarlang?"

The wolf-father paused for effect before speaking. "To destroy the gods utterly, and along with them, the sycophantic worlds they patronize and use for their support. Our kind shall reign from here henceforth. The lowly shall rise above the high, and Asgard shall never have dominion again."

Stunned silence greeted him at first. Then their king stood up, hoisted his hammer in the air, and bellowed a triumphant war-cry of enthusiastic longing. His followers joined him, roaring and waving their thick arms, pounding the ground and the trees. Their eyes shone with hubris and bloodlust.

"Yes!" the king shouted. "I will unleash every horde under my command. We will crash into Asgard's barrier, wave after wave, until it shatters before us!"

Fenris held up a hand. "Not yet, my good king. That would bring the full wrath of the gods down on you before you could breach the divine realm. It would be wiser to keep attacking in safe, limited numbers, enough to distract the deities. Meanwhile, I will weaken them until the final end can be brought about. Once Ragnarök begins, you may attack in full force, overwhelming Asgard and wiping it out of existence."

Again, the trolls cheered. Fenris came over to grasp arms with their king, sealing the bond of agreement.

Before he took his leave, the wolf-father added, "One more thing. You will see me again, and soon. No matter what the circumstances, do not speak of what we've just discussed."

CHAPTER FIVE

Bailey determined that the meat was done, at least well enough. She used magic to turn a piece of stone into a serviceable knife, then carved off a nice big slice. She left the rest still suspended over the fire so that the inner portions would continue to cook.

She was about halfway through her second piece when Fenris emerged from the woods.

"You're alive," she called. "That's usually a good sign."

He approached with an unhurried gait. "Indeed. And it looks like you've begun your meal. I will join you."

The wolf-god pulled some of the inner meat from the elk's thigh. As he sat down beside her, the girl burned with curiosity as to what he'd found on his scouting trip and what the implications would be for them, but she held her tongue, not wanting to seem scared or eager.

Fenris consumed the meat and waited until after he'd licked the juices from his fingers before he began.

"I found their encampment. Another force is amassing

—larger than the first, but manageable. They were making preparations to attack, but not yet marching. I'd estimate that they'll strike soon. Eat, and rest as long as you can. We will need our strength."

That sounded good to Bailey. She had two more big slices of elk meat before she decided she was full, then she stretched and lay back in the snow before the warm fire.

"Fenris," she asked, "will this second wave be the last of them? At least for now?"

He shrugged his broad shoulders. "I cannot say. I saw no signs of more of them, so if we defeat this group, it should buy us time."

They sat in silence for what felt like another half hour, then both of them sat up straight in unison, their ears perking up to the sound of heavy, shuffling footsteps.

Fenris sprang to his feet and waved a clawed hand. "They're coming. Make ready!"

The girl stood beside him, flexing and shifting mental gears toward the kind of instinctual and aggressive thinking required to survive and prevail in a life or death struggle.

Fenris shifted once more into his gigantic wolf-monster form, towering over the snowy plain. Bailey had to admit she felt safer and more confident with him by her side. For a second, she hated herself for doubting him.

The trees shook as dozens of frost trolls streamed out of the shadows between the trunks, roaring and swinging their heavy limbs and crude but deadly weapons in swipes and circles.

As Fenris moved to the left, frantically crushing and

maiming all before him, Bailey took a deep breath and turned to the right half of the invading force. She flung her arms out and unleashed a tidal wave of offensive magic, near the limit of what she was capable of.

Like the shockwave from a nuclear bomb, the storm of magical energy blasted out to engulf the trolls' vanguard. The dozen or so in front died instantly, their bodies collapsing into piles of ash and cinders. The ones behind them survived, but they were wounded and disoriented.

Before Bailey could finish them off, others charged out from around or behind them, seeking to flatten her or tear her limb from limb.

There wasn't time for another all-out arcane assault. She'd have to fight them at close range.

Using telekinesis, the werewitch stole the weapons from her attackers at a distance, summoning a stone axe and crude iron sword into her hands. When she caught them, she realized how massive they were; the handles were nearly too big for her to wrap her fingers around, and they weighed far more than mortal weapons would.

But Bailey was stronger than ever as a deity, and she whipped them around with little effort. She enchanted the rough blades with a mixture of fire and arcane plasma, adding to their damage potential and intimidation factor, then plunged into the trolls' ranks.

A fast swipe of the flaming axe chopped off the arm of the first one to reach her, and she was already bounding over it and through it, the sword slicing through its neck and shoulder area, its body toppling behind her.

She crossed weapons with the next two. The impact of

their swings was incredible, but she'd expected as much and surrounded her arms with an aura of kinetic force. The trolls' clubs shuddered to a halt in midair. Stunned, they could not react in time as Bailey charged between them, slashing the midsections of each as she passed.

A melee followed, during which the girl took multiple stunning, bruising blows and shallow cuts and scratches, but nothing serious, meanwhile dropping eight more of the brutes. She reached an open area, having destroyed the immediate group and penetrated into the no-man's-land between the creatures' ranks. The ones across the snow growled at her but were slow to attack.

Rather than meet them head-on since they were close to the edge of the forest, Bailey thought of something else. She extended her sword hand and channeled the full brunt of her telekinetic ability, uprooting a mass of trees and hurling them into the group of frost trolls.

The beasts howled in alarm as the heavy trunks fell on them, crushing their thick skulls and spines, or rolled into their legs and sent them sprawling. Bailey roared and rushed them, easily finishing off the survivors as she nimbly jumped from tumbling log to tumbling log.

Another cluster emerged from the woods that she'd ravaged. She leapt high in the air, both weapons raised over her head, and came down on a particularly large troll in front who froze and tried to block her with his spear. The enchanted blades passed through the wood and carved the creature into three pieces.

Then the others piled in, surrounding her with a tornado of anger and violence.

She withstood it. Using a mixture of magic and conventional combat, she whittled down their numbers with injuries or death blows until she stood alone on the bloody snow and the last of them ran for the safety of the forest.

Bailey launched herself after him, flying horizontally like a missile, and crashed into the troll's haunches. He tumbled aside and crashed into a tree. The girl came to a stop beside him and raised her axe.

For an instant, she caught a glimpse of his face; it looked almost human and was strained with pain and terror, oddly pitiful. She was still operating on the rush of battle, but part of her didn't want to finish him off like this.

"Hold!" Fenris barked. Having vanquished the rest of the trolls, he had shifted back into his humanoid form. "Allow him to surrender. We might be able to use him."

The girl's hand trembled as she fought down the mindless, aggressive bloodlust that still raged from the long fight. In seconds, breathing deep and forcing a normal state of consciousness to return to her mind, she had herself back under control.

"Okay," she said. "What do we do with him, though?"

Fenris walked over and peered into the troll's big, brutish face. "Do you surrender? And what will you do for us if we let you live?"

The creature gurgled, then its voice rumbled up in halting gasps. "I will…take you…to our king." He shut his eyes, then opened them again. "We can…talk about…surrendering."

The wolf-father leaned back. "Good. Let us go now. Stand up!"

Groaning, the troll struggled to regain his feet, and Bailey helped him. She'd badly damaged some of the muscles in his back when she'd smashed into him. He hobbled into the woods, with Fenris and Bailey close behind.

The girl leaned over to her mentor as the darkness of the forest closed over their heads. "Could he be leading us into a trap?"

"Possibly," Fenris conceded, "but I doubt it."

She had her doubts but decided to trust the god's judgment. The two of them had, after all, defeated more than a hundred of the beasts by themselves.

The trek through the trees took longer than Bailey would have liked, but it was less than an hour before they approached a clearing where the girl could make out many dark silhouettes standing around, as well as the sun glinting off a large object that seemed to be made of ice.

Fenris raised a hand. "This must be it. Yes, I came to the edge of this place earlier. Let me do the talking, Bailey."

"Okay," she agreed.

The girl hung back while Fenris put a hand on the captured troll's neck and guided him into the clearing, where two or three dozen more of their species milled around a throne of ice, on which the biggest troll Bailey had seen lounged. He wore a strange, primitive crown and carried a great hammer. He was obviously their king.

Bailey wondered how many of his personal retinue had participated in the last assault, and how many trolls there might be.

The monsters roiled in their surprise, though a few

simply stared dumbly at Fenris before they reacted. The king glared at him.

"Hail," Fenris began, "King of the frost trolls. We have defeated your warriors and brought this one back to negotiate your surrender, as per the ancient laws of your people."

The king growled and hoisted his warhammer, and Bailey feared that battle was about to break out, but the mood among the trolls was strange and hesitant. They must have known that Fenris spoke the truth about decimating their forces and were afraid of suffering the same fate.

Still, face had to be saved, so the king went through the motions of threatening them and acting haughty, while Fenris issued a mixture of reasonable promises and threats.

As stupid as these trolls supposedly are, Bailey thought, they know a thing or two about negotiations. Maybe we underestimated them. Are they plotting something?

Finally, they reached an agreement.

"So be it," the king grunted. "I will not risk more of my people, brave and strong as we are, on the condition that the forces of Asgard leave us to our own realm and do not seek to expand their own borders into our territory."

"Yes," Fenris replied. "That is acceptable, and we will honor our half of the bargain."

Bailey squinted. She hadn't heard or seen anything to suggest that the Asgardians *were* trying to expand onto frost troll turf, so it must have been a meaningless, symbolic concession, designed to sound like a fair truce rather than an unconditional surrender.

The wounded prisoner stayed behind as Fenris turned

to leave, taking Bailey by the arm and guiding her away from the clearing.

"Wait," she asked. "How do we know that—"

"*Not now*," the wolf-god snapped. "All is well, for the time being."

Angry, the werewitch nevertheless bit her tongue until they were a fair distance from the trolls and presumably out of earshot.

"Okay, then," she inquired again. "If it's safe, how do we know that they'll keep their side of the deal and follow the new policy or whatever?"

Fenris grimaced. "We don't know. Not for certain. But I have no reason to believe they'll try anything soon. My best guess is that they will lie low for a time, licking their wounds and recouping their losses, then look for some minor technicality that can be used against us to 'justify' a resumption of hostilities."

She frowned. "Ugh. That sucks."

As they emerged from the woods, Fenris elaborated. "Of late, many creatures have grown strangely impatient to start Ragnarök—to attack Asgard and the gods, attempting to overthrow them, triggering the End of Days, which they feel will lead to a new age when they will rule. It is difficult to say what lies ahead, but we must be cautious and ready for anything."

Bailey went cold.

He knows about it, then. He's aware that something is wrong, and he didn't seem scared or angry when he said that. What are his real goals and intentions? How the hell can I be sure of anything anymore?

Their elk was still waiting for them by the campfire.

The second battle had, absurdly enough, spared it. The pair sat down by the blaze, which had burned down to mostly coals at this point, and Fenris added another log from the debris of fractured trees that lay strewn across the plain.

Fenris tore into the carcass again as Bailey roasted some strips threaded on sticks, sitting and watching the forest. Waiting, guarded, and prepared for betrayal.

Roland raised his hands to get everyone to shut up. "All right, pipe down. We're all assembled, and you all understand what's at stake. Right?"

Dante, at his side, added, "We don't have a lot of time to answer tons of questions, but we do want to make sure that anyone who comes along understands what they're getting into. This isn't going to be a cakewalk."

Watching his friend, Roland saw Dante exchange meaningful glances with Charlene, his girlfriend, who stood among the group of two dozen witches they'd recruited.

At present, they were gathered in an empty field a mile outside the Portland suburbs, near the foothills of the Cascades. The two wizards had decided to do most of their recruitment drive in the City of Roses, since it was far closer to Greenhearth than Seattle was, not to mention it was Portland witches who'd fed the worst of Callie's undead hunger. Charlene had come down from Seattle to be by her lover's side in the battle to come. Deanna, another woman who'd helped them against Aradia, losing her friend Shari in the fight, had come, too.

Two witches, a young man, and a slightly older woman,

raised their hands, and the woman spoke. "How many of these things are there again?" she inquired. "And if they can replicate themselves, then how will attacking small pockets of them do much good? I'm not saying I don't want to help, only that I'd rather do something that *does* help instead of just pissing them off."

Murmurs went through the shuffling crowd.

Dante sighed. "That's a valid point. The idea is, they can only replicate themselves so fast, and they need to feed on mortal witches in order to do that, so if the bulk of them are holed up in this canyon in the Other, then obviously they can't do it. We'll be hitting them when and where they're weak."

Half the casters nodded, but the others still looked unsure.

Roland raised a finger. "Oh, and also, the Agency has these new weapons that not only disperse the crones' energy but also sucks up their essence into these little tanks, which prevents them from reconstituting themselves. So with them fighting with us, we'll be able to tear through them pretty well. The big danger is that we can't afford to provoke the entire horde at once and get surrounded, and we've all been planning extensively on how to avoid that."

This seemed to mostly satisfy the witches. Roland glossed over a couple more questions, answering in vague terms and pledging that the agents would be able to fill in the rest when the time came. Which he hoped was true.

"Okay," he concluded, "let's go. The sooner we hit them, the better."

The group piled into their convoy of vehicles and made

for the highway. They headed southeast into the mountains, arriving in Greenhearth about forty-five or fifty minutes later. Roland had come in his Audi, with Dante riding shotgun, and he led the group down side streets and then rough, bumpy dirt road that led to the abandoned farm owned by the Nordin family, where everyone would be gathering.

The Agency's task force was already there, waiting for them in front of the old barn.

This, Roland recalled, *was where Bailey was going to hide me from Shannon and Aida and Callie, except that prick Dan Oberlin and his boys found us instead. That was our first fight together.*

As the witches emerged from their cars, Roland saw with gut-roiling disappointment that Velasquez and Park had procured all of ten other agents to join them. On the plus side, the dozen were bristling with weapons and armor and looked like they were mostly elite black-ops guys, which he regarded as a good sign.

And yet, that's three dozen of us versus, what, five hundred or so of them? He shook his head.

Velasquez approached. "Glad you could make it. Is this everyone?"

"Yup," said Dante. "Is this everyone?" He looked at the agents' squad. "We're a tad short of an *army,* aren't we?"

Park grimaced. "Yeah, well, quality over quantity. These guys are the best, I hear."

The senior agent concurred. "Yes, they were all with us when we took on Aradia. They have experience fighting in the Other and using this kind of high-level equipment. I would have liked to garner more men, but the Agency has its fingers in a lot of different pies right now, and our fearless leaders never seem to grasp the magnitude of a threat until the shitstorm begins in full force. We have to make do with what we have."

Behind Roland, the witches muttered; they'd been expecting a larger group of allies, too.

"Yeah, whatever," the wizard responded, trying to sound confident. "The talent and technology we've got here should be enough. Now, let's get 'em. Are we going to the same place?"

Velasquez had ambled off to fire up the gateway device, so Park answered.

"Not quite. We'll be dropping on a shelf of rock on the other side of the canyon that has easier access to the crones' gathering place via multiple routes. After we do some quick reconnaissance, that will allow us more opportunities to divide and conquer the fuckers while still having routes of escape if we provoke too many of them at once."

Deanna quipped, "Well, good thing you guys have a well-thought-out strategy. Let's do this."

Velasquez had set the gateway device up within the barn, and after he punched in the coordinates, it glowed purple before growing a portal within its central section. "We're good," he announced. "Come on."

He and five other agents went through first, followed by the two dozen witches, with the remaining Agency guys bringing up the rear.

They emerged into a small red valley filled with boulders and gravel. Three paths that all looked traversable on foot wound out of the hollow and into the low, jagged mountains. The canyon, Roland guessed, must lay beyond.

Velasquez assumed command of the overall operation. He dispatched three men to scout the paths, then turned to face the rest of the group.

"They say you should never divide your forces," he opened, "but 'never' is a strong word. In this case, we're going to break up into three squads, each consisting of a dozen men or women, eight witches and four agents. Witches with talent at shielding will be out in front, followed by the agents, then the other witches in the rear. The idea is to locate and engage with small pockets of the crones, lure them away from the others, and destroy them systematically for as long as we can get away with."

The scouts returned, reporting that two of the three paths led into the canyon. The other didn't seem to, but they had glimpsed a cluster of ten or twelve crones, maybe more, within a side hollow down there.

Velasquez nodded. "Split up. Our agents will be in communication with one another. Let the remaining groups know as soon as you engage the enemy or if anything goes wrong. Move."

Roland found himself in a group alongside Deanna and four agents he didn't know. They would be handling the leftmost path, the one that was supposedly a dead end. Dante and Charlene were in Velasquez's squad, which would tackle the central path. Park led the one taking the right-hand path.

They set off at a fast march and clambered over the rough, stony ground, working their way first up out of the valley and then down the bluff toward the huge gorge, bits of which Roland could see between the spires of rock before them.

They'd gone half a mile when the agent in command raised a hand for them to stop. "This was where I saw them," he whispered and gestured at an open space up ahead, just past a slight bend in the trail.

Roland went out in front, along with a female witch whose name he'd forgotten—Linda or Laura or Lena, something like that. He'd never met her, but she claimed to be an accomplished shielder.

Creeping forward, they spotted the wafting rags of the crones before the creatures saw them. Roland conjured a pair of invisible shields to protect most of the space between the two groups but left an opening in the center for the lead agents to fire through.

Everyone held their breath.

Green beams blazed out of the agents' disruptor rifles, transforming the four eldritch crones in front into masses of sparkling particles. The rest of the undead clones streamed toward them, raking their claws in the air and howling like banshees.

Roland cursed the noise as he and the woman beside him deflected a series of nasty magical attacks. Behind him, one of the agents quickly reported into his headpiece that they'd engaged the crones. The witches in the rear hurled further attacks at their foes' heads.

It was over in a minute or so. As with the group Roland, Dante, and the two agents had fought before, the engagement was brief but intense. It occurred to the wizard that Callie's clones did not possess full human intelligence. Not surprising; Callie hadn't been terribly smart.

"Hell, yes," the agent with the headpiece gloated. "Okay, blue team reporting. We neutralized the threat here. There doesn't appear to be a further path toward the canyon that we can reach, so we're heading back to the hub valley. Over."

Velasquez approved the course of action once the agents finished vacuuming up the crones' lingering essence. The squad returned to their point of entry. During their brief trek, Park's group reported that it had easily defeated fourteen or fifteen crones as well, meaning that the mortals had vanquished maybe thirty of the creatures thus far.

No sooner had they arrived than Velasquez was back on the headset, demanding they reinforce his group. They'd stumbled onto a broad slope leading into the main canyon and were under attack by hundreds of crones.

"Shit," Roland muttered. "Either we're going to have to abort prematurely, or we get to reenact the goddamn Battle of Thermopylae."

"What?" someone asked.

"You know," Roland replied, "like in the movie *300*. A small group defends a narrow pass from a horde that's a couple hundred times bigger than they are."

A few people chuckled at the implied badassery, but then everyone remembered that all the Spartans had died in the end.

Roland's group rushed down the central path, finding it flatter and easier to navigate than the left trail had been. It wasn't long until they heard the sounds of combat and saw flashing lights, then Velasquez's squad came into sight.

The wizard saw with tremendous relief that they hadn't

lost anyone yet. Dante and Charlene were visible at the rear, and the agents' green disruptor beams were wreaking massive havoc. At least a hundred crones had massed at the far end of the visible trail and were pouring into the crevasse, wailing hideously in unison.

Deanna gasped. "This might be worse than fighting Aradia. We only had fifty enemies to deal with, and we had another goddess on our side."

Roland couldn't agree more. As they joined the other group and began hurling spells toward the colossal mass of undead abominations, he only hoped that wherever the hell Bailey was, she was safe.

And preferably almost done with whatever she's doing, his mind added. *We could kinda use her help.*

Bailey could no longer stand it. She had to ask him.

"Fenris," she piped up as he sat glowering at the trolls' forest, "do you think Ragnarök is coming? The old legends say it's inevitable that it'll happen sooner or later, don't they?"

By now, the light had faded. The realm of the frost trolls did not seem to have a proper "night," but the omnipresent illumination grew soft and dim and bluish, as opposed to the bright whiteness that had surrounded them earlier. A gentle snow fell from the sky.

The wolf-father turned to her. "Possibly," he rumbled, with a vague swipe of his hand. His face was hidden under his hood. "The legends are interpretations of interpretations, mostly by mortals. They are not always correct, but they usually contain a seed of truth. Many creatures throughout the cosmos *believe* that Ragnarök is foretold and must happen, and because they believe it, their own actions are more likely to make it happen."

She opted to try a different tack and see how her mentor would react to a firm statement instead of a question.

"Well," she said, "if that's the way it is, we need to stop it one way or another."

Fenris's solemn scowl changed into what looked like a faint, sad smile. "You're so determined and confident. I have always liked that about you, Bailey. But if such a thing awaits us, stopping it will be...difficult, to put it mildly."

"Difficult," she queried, "or impossible? There's a big difference between the two. You taught me that as much as anyone else."

He shook his head. "I do not know, but if it is possible, you and I are up to the task. We have cleared every other hurdle, and heretofore defeated all our adversaries. We've always been able to do what must be done."

She smiled, and despite her suspicions, it was genuine. "Yes. We make a hell of a team."

They'd eaten most of the dead elk, and only bones, cartilage, and skin remained. The girl was amazed that they'd been able to put away so much meat, but they were gods, and this wasn't Earth.

Fenris stood up. "We should spar. I want to test your abilities once more."

After their long rest and filling meal, Bailey had found that she was refreshed and relaxed, not to mention bored.

She jumped to her feet. "Sure. What abilities? I've got a lot of them."

He chuckled at that. "I know. In our recent battle with the trolls, I noticed that you did not shift. I'd like to see your wolf form and ensure you can still fight as well on four legs as two."

She made a sour face. "It's easier to do magic in human form. I can do it as a wolf, but it takes more mental effort, and even then, I can't seem to hit the same heights of power."

"I see." He stretched his limbs and flung off his coat. "Yet you fought more with your body than your arcane capabilities. The lupine form is better for melee combat. Now, shift!"

As he spoke, he grew and changed, his clothes shredding as, for the third time, he took on the shape of a wolf-creature the size of a farmhouse. Examining him up close like this in the eerie blue light of the realm's strange extended twilight, he looked both impressive and monstrously sinister.

Bailey inhaled, then shifted. To her surprise, her own clothes fell away too; a couple months ago, she'd altered her wolf form to be smaller so her wardrobe would stay mostly intact from one form to another.

But now she was bigger. There was the familiar lengthening of body, the sprouting of hair, the reddish sheen from her eyes that encompassed her vision. She grew even larger than the first time she'd ever changed, swelling to the size of a pickup truck.

When Fenris spoke, it was a psychic rumble she heard with her mind instead of her ears. That did not shock her since she'd communicated with her pack via a similar telepathy.

Good, he said, *but you are not as far along as you should be.*

She was puzzled. *What do you mean?*

The wolf-god circled her, regarding her with his dark indigo eyes the way a natural wolf might evaluate a deer. *Later. For the moment, fight!*

He pounced. She dodged, knowing she couldn't confront his greater mass directly, but despite his size, he was every bit as fast as she was. Fenris spun in mid-air, and their teeth and claws lashed out.

Bailey fell back, bleeding from superficial cuts, then pounced on her mentor's furry front leg. Her teeth dug into it, and she sought to pull him off balance.

He spun, dragging her through the snow and finally hurling her a hundred yards through the air to crash into a drift by the trees. When she sprang back to her feet, he was bounding toward her, though his left front leg was noticeably lame from her attack.

Once more the two beasts clashed, Bailey fighting as furiously as she could and inflicting multiple wounds on Fenris, but she could not defeat him. He was larger, stronger, and more experienced, and the efforts of continuing such a lopsided battle wore her down.

Finally he batted her aside with his shoulder, stepped on her stomach, and poised his fangs to rip out her throat.

Is he really going to do it? she wondered, abruptly terrified.

He did not. He dropped back on his haunches, looked at her evenly, and then changed back into a man, his hooded coat magically reconstituted over his body.

Panting, the girl rose to four feet, then two. It took her a second to remember that she was naked, but after a moment of concentration, she retrieved the scraps of her clothes and repaired them through mental sorcery.

"We will need rest," Fenris stated, "since we gave each other several nasty wounds. As deities, the healing will be quick."

She nodded and fell on her rump by the fire, surprised by how exhausted she felt.

Fenris came over to her and placed a hand on her shoulder. "When I said you were not as far along as you ought to be, what I meant was that in this realm, your size as a wolf reflects your stature as a divine being. You've grown as a goddess, so your lycanthropic form is bigger, but you are still not yet ready."

She held his gaze. "Ready for what?"

He did not answer right away or directly. Instead, he looked off toward the horizon, where the light seemed to be brightening as the dimension's pseudo-night reached its end.

"It is my hope," he explained, "that you will rise to my stature. New possibilities will open up, and our universe will be far better with another entity like me."

He began talking more about the practice and focus she'd need to continue improving, and his projections of when the trolls might break the truce. The girl tried to listen and nod her head and offer minor, banal comments when she could.

But within her mind, a single thought kept repeating. What he'd said about wanting her to be exactly like him had set off a cold, nauseated sinking sensation within her that did not lessen as long as the notion screamed in her brain.

It's true, what Loki said. There's no other reason he'd want me to be his equal since everyone says not to train your replacement unless replacement is the point. It's all fucking true.

Loki smiled as he reclined in his chair in the great, airy crystal chamber that looked out upon blue skies and clouds—the council's meeting room, where he'd not sat since before Fenris had attempted to murder him. It saddened him that he hadn't been able to vote in Bailey's trial.

Though apparently his son, having assumed his form, had voted the way he would have, with a "yea."

Thoth, the Egyptian god of wisdom, raised his hands as his eyes glimmered beneath his ibis headdress. He usually acted as the council's spokesman and mediator, thus coming closer than anyone to being its leader, though officially, all six members were of equal rank.

"So," he intoned, continuing the conversation that had been going on for quite some time, "we are all satisfied that there is no deception here. That everyone is who they claim and appear to be, and that Fenris is far away and unaware of our having convened."

Heads nodded. Since Bailey, who'd taken over Freya's

seat, was not present, the only other deities in the room besides Loki and Thoth were Thor, Norse god of thunder and war, Balder, Norse god of beauty and innocence, and Coyote, the good-natured trickster god of the Western American tribes.

"And," Coyote chimed in, "with Fenris safely gone, I'm afraid there's no denying the truth anymore, is there? For all her intemperance of late, Freya was right."

Thor put a hand to his eyes and shook his head. "Aye. I scarce want to believe it, but it's true: Loki's bastard means to start Ragnarök. I didn't think he was *that* mad. I should've known something was wrong, though, when he insisted on dealing with this stupid frost troll incursion by himself. Normally he would have *preferred* to have Mjölnir and me by his side! No troll can stand before my mighty hammer!"

Balder shook his head, ignoring Thor's extraneous comment. "I, too, would have expected better of him, despite my listening to Freya at first. But the evidence is against him. He has moved against *us* with killing intent, and his activities with regard to Bailey and other things have been most suspicious. What he is doing in the trolls' realm should be investigated in more detail."

Thoth nodded. "Exactly what Fenris hopes to accomplish by this, I cannot say. You of the Norse pantheon, this deals more with your domain, yet I fear that the consequences will spill far beyond your purview. Other divine pantheons could be involved, damaged, or altered beyond recognition. The destruction that will rage might easily affect the world of mortals and possibly destroy it altogether. Even if other gods are left alone, the obliteration of so many of their followers would leave them weakened and change our universe to the point of devastation."

Loki sat in silence, listening to the other deities finally grasp what he had long suspected, and what his son had confirmed the day he'd tried to kill him. Loki had allowed him to *think* he'd succeeded. It had been perhaps the cleverest, or at least the wisest, thing he'd ever done.

Balder asked, "But what can we do? We might be able to attack and kill him, but it's possible that the things he's set in motion could proceed without him. And with Fenris dead, we may not be able to learn what his plans are in time to stop them."

Coyote offered, "We should rely upon Bailey for now. She's close to him. Perhaps too close; Loki says she was hostile and skeptical about his accusations. Yet if nothing else, we might be able to get important information from her without seeming to move too aggressively."

The gods all agreed to this, but none of them could offer a further solution. There was a dreadful hesitancy in them all, a sense that things might be slipping beyond their control.

Loki raised his hand. "I have a suggestion."

Thoth looked at him. "Oh? Speak, Loki."

The Norse god of mischief smiled and flexed his hands, satisfied at the notion that he was the most knowledgeable person in the chamber regarding the situation at hand.

"What we should do," he told them, "is take turns shadowing Fenris. Following him, observing but not directly intervening. If we can guess what his next move is, then we can get ahead of him and sabotage him in advance or do things to distract him and draw him off, slowing down his timetable."

No one objected, and Loki continued before any could interrupt. "And that's only the half of it. The other half deals with Bailey. While one of us, regardless of which one, trails Fenris and keeps him away from the girl, others can meet with her privately and begin instructing her in the part she might have to play."

Thoth rubbed his broad, dark chin as the others' eyes grew distant with contemplation.

"You see," Loki went on, "Fenris's plans hinge on Bailey. He requires her in order to bring his little scheme to fruition, so she is his weak point. For us to move against him could cause unnecessarily messy ripples throughout the cosmos, not to mention make him desperate enough to try something even more ridiculous than what he's done so far. But if the werewitch can resist him, that might wrap things up rather more easily."

The gods agreed.

"Aye," said Thor. "I'll teach her battle, and the rest of you can teach her further magical techniques or ways of thinking and perceiving things like a proper god. Obviously, she's got some talent in all those things, but she'll need more."

No one objected.

Raising his hands again, Thoth proclaimed, "It is settled, then. We shall draw lots to see who shadows Fenris unless someone wishes to volunteer. The others of us will prepare a program to instruct Bailey to be our instrument. Let us decide who will do what first, then we shall depart and begin."

Leaving Bailey to rest by the remains of their fire as daybreak brightened the cold landscape, Fenris set off again into the woods. He shifted into wolf form as soon as he was out of the girl's sight, covering an enormous distance at a run, and quickly found the clearing of the frost troll king's icy throne.

"Fenris," the monarch greeted him, his beady eyes narrowed with suspicion. "We played along, but what was the purpose of that? You cannot be both my friend and my enemy!"

The wolf-god raised a hand palm outward in a gesture of appeasement. "I understand, great king. You must realize that the girl cannot know what we mean to do. Not yet, anyhow. This temporary 'surrender' of yours is the best way forward."

Trolls of the king's retinue snarled under their breath. They clearly wanted to fight and regarded the truce as humiliating or nonsensical. Fortunately, their leader was smarter than they were.

Fenris explained, "It will keep Bailey on her toes, looking for further threats from you or elsewhere, thus distracting her from the rest of our endeavors. At the same time, she will think that she and I won an honest victory here and that all is well, for the most part. I have no reason to suspect she knows the truth."

"Fine," the king barked. "But why is she so important? I've never seen or heard of her. And what would you have us do now that we are bound not to attack?"

The wolf-father tried not to laugh at the troll's density.

"The girl is crucial; I will say no more than that. As for your part to play, the farce of your supposed surrender provides you with a certain amount of cover. As long as you do not directly attack Asgard again, everyone will assume you've been beaten and are in no condition to fight. In fact, their watchful eyes will grow sleepy, and you will find it easier to marshal the bulk of your forces for the real battle to come."

The troll monarch tilted his head as full understanding dawned, and it trickled down to his subordinates, who grinned with savage triumph at the thought of having fooled the gods.

"Yes," the king rasped. "I will raise the mightiest army in the history of our world!"

Fenris nodded. "Do so, your majesty. Rally every troll you can find who is willing or able to fight. Marshal them in force, with the best weapons you have, train them in combat, and drum up their bloodlust. The time is coming soon."

A few of the creatures hoisted clubs and spears and axes into the air in response to his words, their eyes gleaming.

"And," Fenris went on, "when the day *does* come, we shall have our revenge. The gods, languishing in their fat and lazy stupor, will be caught unaware. We will unleash hell and take Asgard, reducing it to ruin and rubble."

Trolls jumped up and down, beating fists to their broad chests, and the king, grinning with fantasies of red victory, invited Fenris to stay for an impromptu feast.

He agreed. The trolls made a smooth circle in the snow in which to sit and brought out a flat-topped rock for the wolf-god to use as a chair. Then they roasted an assortment of meats and paired them with a foul-tasting but potent liquor fermented from winter plants that lay beyond Fenris's knowledge.

As the congregation ate and drank, the wolf-god, sitting by the king's right hand, engaged his ally in conversation.

"Fenris," the huge troll-leader asked in a low voice, unheard by his rowdy minions, "I like your plan. But my men are not smart enough to know how easily it can go wrong. The gods are not as lazy as you say. They will notice what is happening and oppose us. How do we deal with them before they can stop us?"

The renegade deity stroked his stubbled chin beneath his hood. "There are ways. I do not know yet how we will remove them, but it can be done, and it will. I have several ideas but must remain flexible rather than committing to any of them. There is something important to consider."

The king leaned closer.

Fenris took a drink of the troll's powerful liquor and breathed in through his flaring nostrils. "The prophecies are both clear and adamant about certain things. It is of absolute necessity that we destroy both Balder and Tyr."

The monarch raised a shaggy eyebrow.

"Tyr," Fenris explained, "does not sit upon the council, but he is far from untouchable, and his presence can be required, in one way or another if we require it. He, the god of justice, must die along with the god of beauty. Only with both of them wiped out can Ragnarök proceed."

"Aye," the king agreed. "If we can help you slay them, we will. But what of Thor? He is the one who worries us most. He's killed untold numbers of our people with his hammer, curse him!"

The wolf-father waved a hand dismissively. "He is not of great concern. For all his might and readiness to charge into battle, he is doomed. I will leave him for Jormungandr, the World Serpent. It is that creature's destiny to fight and slay him. If all goes well, the gods shall die, and in the new world, it will be beasts who reign."

He tore into another strip of meat with his teeth, his ancient mind playing out all the scenarios of what might occur as his hulking ally quaffed another flagon of liquor.

"Good," said the king. "Great! This is what we've waited for through generations of patient anger. The gods should never have ruled. The world has always been ours!"

Fenris smiled, though deep in his mind, he did not agree. Most of what he'd told the troll-monarch a moment ago was true to his intentions. A new world was coming, and creatures who had long hidden in its shadows would now stride free across its broad avenues and sit in its high places.

But Fenris had long-term aspirations. Asgard deserved to fall; the pantheon was owed its destruction. Still, he was a part of that pantheon, and with its residual wisdom as his heritage, he, having survived the conflict, would be better qualified than any other entity to act as sovereign over all creation.

Roland pushed his shield back, forcing two of the shrieking ghost-crones along with it and directly into the path of an agent's disruptor rifle. Their corpse-like faces lengthened in horror as the green plasma tore them apart, only for their residues to be sucked into the agents' wrist-tanks.

Dante laughed beside him. "Is it just me, or are these things a lot stupider and weaker than Callie was?"

"They are," Roland confirmed, "but they're still danger-ous, and we've only made a dent in them, so don't celebrate too soon."

The two combined squads of mortals in the central pathway had retreated after eliminating the initial wave-attack of crones and rejoined the third squad at a juncture-point between paths. There, the three-dozen-strong force made their stand against the onslaught of the undead clones.

And by Roland's estimate, they'd destroyed a minimum of one hundred and fifty of the things, while losing none of their own number. Combat against the creatures was growing routine, to the point that he was getting tired of looking at so many incarnations of Caldoria McCluskey, borderline unrecognizable though she was.

Yet they'd been fighting for an hour and a half to two hours. Channeling magic in the Other required more effort than using it back on Earth; the casters were all growing drained of strength.

The agents began to complain that their weapons were running low. They had to rotate half their men to the rear to recharge their guns enough to use them for another five minutes, then cycle those guys forward while the others repeated the process.

Velasquez, falling back from the blazing chaos and noise of the front line, shouted, "We need to retreat. Too much fatigue and not enough power in our weapons to handle all these things. Good news is that they are doing the same thing."

He pointed, and Roland squinted to follow his finger.

It was true; of the crones who'd initially pursued them up the path, most had turned back to join the main congregation. That left a mere two dozen or so who continued to fight.

"Okay, fine," Roland countered, "we'll finish these off and then head back to camp or whatever."

Sucking in air, he launched himself back into battle, mostly playing defense to the other witches or the agents, but occasionally getting in a lightning bolt or fireball of his own.

The crones, for their part, fought mindlessly but with great ferocity, spitting out a limited number of unimaginative but dangerous spells. In some cases, they paused to try to siphon energy from the witches, but the ones who attempted it were destroyed before they could accomplish much.

Finally, the last of them was disintegrated and vacuumed up, and the three dozen tired combatants began a defensive retreat back to the hub valley.

"Hold," Velasquez called as they entered the hollow. "We're not going home yet. Instead, we're camping at this portal. Yes, camping, like in a fucking video game. The things know we're here, and I suspect they'll come after us before they worry about opening other portals back to Earth and trying that shit. If we hold this point, we can keep picking them off."

A few of the casters frowned or grumbled at this, and Roland wondered if they'd thought this would be a mere two- or three-hour errand, rather than the multi-day expedition it might shape up to be. He should have been clearer with them.

But they'd needed everyone they could get.

The witches watched curiously as the agents set up silver-chrome poles at the edges of the three passageways leading out of the valley toward the canyon. Once activated, the poles generated a pale, transparent curtain of purplish light stretching between them.

Velasquez gestured toward it. "That's an arcane energy reversal field," he exposited. "Not the same as what our guns fire, but it will block spectral beings from passing through unless they have a death wish. As such, we'll be safe for a while, and this valley should remain a clear zone as long as those things are up. Later we can portal back here and use this place as a staging zone for further incursions."

Since they'd be taking a break to rest and recharge their armaments, Velasquez also decided to let everyone eat. He ordered Park to distribute a couple packs' worth of Meals, Ready-to-Eat that the Agency had purchased from the Department of Defense.

Park grinned evilly. "Any of you people ever had an MRE before? Hoo, boy! Are you ever in for the complete opposite of a treat!"

"I have," a male witch said. "Army Infantry, 2012 to 2016. They're not *that* bad. I mean, they've gotten better since my dad was in the service, based on the shit he said. I was kind of a fan of the ravioli, to be honest."

Park snorted. "If all you ever eat is microwaveable junk or crap out of cans, I guess they're okay. But clearly, you've never had my mom's authentic Korean cooking, have you?"

The guy shrugged. "So, invite me to dinner when this is all over."

"I may," Park retorted. "She lives in Los Angeles, though."

"Oh," the other man muttered. "Fuck that, then."

They all tore into the packaged meals and found mostly an assortment of macaroni and cheese, meatloaf, and decently-preserved vegetables. Roland found his tolerable, but he could understand why deployed military personnel tended to find themselves missing home cooking or proper restaurants very quickly.

The agents also set up a portable heating device. According to Velasquez, they could have made a fire without fear, since the crones were not as devious as human opponents, but there was nothing to burn. The landscape was totally devoid of wood.

Roland and Dante sat about halfway back from the heater. Being from Seattle, they didn't much mind the Other's chill, though the agents from California, Nevada, and Arizona seemed uncomfortable.

Dante shook his head as he finished his meal. "I still don't understand how the heck this happened. Like, how did it occur to her to make that many copies of herself? You said she wasn't the sharpest tool in the shed originally. Something must have 'clicked' after those wraiths turned her into an eldritch crone."

Roland shrugged. "Yeah, it's bizarre. Her main form, the body that possessed her consciousness that we obliterated a week or two ago? That must have been a distraction while she kept parsing off her essence into all these things. She must have been feeding, unseen and unknown, for a long period of time before she moved up to killing people and got our attention."

"Probably," the younger wizard agreed. "The thing is, there has to be something else anchoring and protecting these clones. They're inferior copies, phantoms of phantoms, so according to basic magical theory as I understand it, they should have faded or collapsed in on themselves by this point." He frowned. "Though, admittedly, I don't claim to know everything about everything."

Roland, who was well versed in arcane knowledge for his age, allowed his eyes to go distant as his mind raced ahead. "No, Dante, I think you're right."

Park and another agent who'd been passing by stopped.

"What do you mean?" Park asked. Other agents and witches glanced toward them as well.

Raising his voice to address the whole group, Roland explained, "There has to be, uh, like a magical device of some sort empowered with the essence of Callie—the original crone—rooting all these duplicates to physical or semi-physical existence. By themselves, they're relatively weak, and their advantage is clearly in numbers."

"Right," an agent agreed.

"So," Roland continued, "since they're pale shadows of the power she had before, they'd scatter or melt into nothing without something holding them together. I can't say what it is or where to look for it. Maybe down there, surrounded by hundreds of the goddamn things, maybe someplace different. But there must be a way..."

Velasquez came over. "I'm not expert on this shit, but what you say makes sense. I'll pass it on to the eggheads. Any bright ideas would be helpful at this point."

Eerie howling approached, and the men and women looked to see another mass of eldritch specters crowding up against the purple barrier between the poles. Thirty or forty of them had come from the central and right-hand paths.

"For fuck's sake," Deanna groaned.

Velasquez ordered them to make ready to confront the crones. After a short warm-up and a brief conference on tactics, as well as double-checking to ensure their rifles were charged, the agents and witches pushed through the barrier and immediately engaged their foes.

Since they had to fight at closer range than before, two witches took nasty burns on their arms and legs, and one agent was dashed against the stone wall of the pass, where he cracked a rib. They didn't lose anyone, though, and were able to annihilate the phantoms in a matter of minutes.

"Good," Velasquez stated. "Move the poles into the passages. We're extending our safe zone. This way, we can use these paths to get closer to the canyon and observe what's going on down there unmolested."

Once the task was done, the senior agent seemed loath to press any further attacks.

"We don't have the manpower or firepower," he pointed out. "The fact that we took minor casualties at close range demonstrates the fuckery that will happen if anyone gets cut off and surrounded by two hundred of the things at once, which is a real possibility if we try to fight the whole horde with a goddamn platoon's worth of people."

"Okay," Charlene acceded. "What should we do, then?"

Velasquez pursed his lips and smoothed his black hair. "We, meaning the Agency personnel, will stay here and hold the fort. I want you guys, the casters, to go home and tell all your friends to come along for the ride. Or better yet…"

Roland held up a hand, palm flatly outwards. "Say no more. If she's back, we'll get her. If she isn't back, I'll file a formal complaint with management about how she's neglecting her duties as a goddess."

Bailey opened a portal and stared into the irregular amethyst-hued surface. Snow continued to fall around her from the dim blue light, the "day" of the trolls' domain having changed again to "night."

"Well, Fenris," she mumbled, though the wolf-god was not present, "if you need me—and I know you do—you know where to find me."

She'd waited long enough for him to return. She stepped through the gateway, and the usual chill was accompanied by another, deeper chill as she realized that the idea of him *needing* her had acquired a new meaning.

The slight dizziness of astral travel passed, and she found herself standing on the slope behind her backyard as usual. Leaning against the wall of the pole barn were Roland and Dante.

"Well," her fiancé began, standing up straight when he saw her. "Who's this chick, and what's she doing on Nordin family property? You're trespassing, young lady."

She strode over to him and slugged him gently in the stomach. He doubled over slightly and let out an *oof*.

"You know damn well who I am, dork. Hi, Dante. Sorry I took off so fast, but it was an emergency. Goddess shit; you know how it goes. Fenris had to fetch me in the middle of the night."

Dante waved. "Hi, Bailey."

Roland stood back up and made a show of massaging his abdomen. "We had something of an emergency ourselves. The Men in Black—or Men in Dark Grayish-Green, whatever—came to fetch us, albeit in the middle of the day. So there. Unfortunately, the emergency is still going on, but before we get to that..."

He grabbed her, wrapped his arms around her, and

pressed her body to his, kissing first her forehead and then her mouth. She didn't complain.

She brushed his nose with the tip of her own. "I missed you."

"Ditto." He kissed her cheek for good measure. "Is everything okay?"

She closed her eyes and nodded. "For the time being, I guess. Fenris...shit, I dunno what to think anymore. He helped me again, I'll say that much. I can tell you about it later. First I need food. I ate half an elk, but I'm kinda feeling the need to go to the other Elk if you don't mind."

Roland looked at Dante. "Is that okay with you? Fine with me. Better than military-grade MREs in any event."

The three Nordin brothers were already at the Bristling Elk, having lunch and beers, so going there killed two proverbial birds with one stone.

When they arrived, the trio sought out Jacob, Russell, and Kurt, finding them at their usual booth.

"Oh, hi!" Jacob greeted them. "Goddamn, Bailey, we were worried as all hell."

She frowned. "I know, and I apologize. It was an emergency. Let's move a table over so I can order myself a steak sandwich."

While they waited for their food, they chatted sporadically about minor bullshit. Bailey did not feel much like talking about all that had happened while she was gone, and Roland and Dante didn't regale her with the tale of what they'd been up to, either. It wasn't until the sandwiches arrived and everyone dug in that they resumed discussion of serious matters.

"So," the werewitch began through a mouthful of steak,

cheese, bread, and sauce, "the gist of what I was doing is that some pricks from another dimension were trying to invade Asgard—Fenris's home turf, basically—and we had to *convince* them to stop. Which we did, mostly. Another time, I'll tell you the details."

Kurt cracked his neck. "Ohhh. *Convince* them. Like how you convinced Aradia to stop existing, I'm guessing?"

"Yeah," the girl confirmed, "though it wasn't as elaborate. Roland, you said there was something important still going on. Fill me in."

Breathing deeply, he and Dante related all that had happened. All four of the Nordins gawked in amazement as they went on.

Jacob whistled. "A Grand Canyon's worth of floating zombie witches from Hell. Things keep getting better and better, don't they?"

Dante said, "They *will* get better if our plan has any basis in reality, which it probably does because we're smart."

"Exactly," Roland confirmed. "However, we're not as strong as, you know, a deity. With Bailey's muscle on our side, we're pretty sure we can figure out the rest of what we need to learn and rid the world of Caldoria McCluskey once and for all. God, it feels good to say that."

Bailey swallowed the last of her sandwich. "I bet." She sighed, realizing that she could do with a night's sleep even though the arcane realms refreshed her without the need for traditional slumber. There was a kind of compound mental tiredness that had nothing to do with the needs of the body, and she felt it now.

Dante pointed out, "The agents are waiting. Time is different in there, but we shouldn't delay too long."

"Yeah, yeah." Bailey grunted. "Let me finish my coffee, then I'll join you guys in saving my second world in two days. Tomorrow maybe I'll save two worlds in *one* day, then take Saturday off."

Russell put his huge hand over hers. "Bailey. If you need us, say the word. And don't work too hard."

Usually Russell wasn't the sentimental type, so she knew he meant it. Jacob and Kurt echoed what the middle brother had said, and she embraced them all before she departed with the two wizards.

Roland drove. "The good news," he quipped, "is that having been to this weird-ass part of the Other where the Callies are gathering, I can portal back instead of relying on the Agency's oh-so-fancy technology."

"Well," Dante observed, "it *is* fancy. And it works!"

Roland narrowed his eyes. "Silence."

Once back at the house, the older wizard opened the gateway in the rear of the pole barn, as Velasquez had done with his device earlier. "Oh," he added, "Charlene and Deanna are there too, if you remember them."

Bailey nodded. In fact, she barely recognized the names, which made her feel strangely ashamed. She wanted to care about all the people in her life, everyone under her divine purview as the goddess of witches and Weres. But there were so many of them, and so much had happened lately. Her brain was overflowing.

They stepped through the portal and into the desolate valley.

"Hi!" Roland announced as all eyes turned toward them. "We have successfully procured the goddess."

"Yup," Dante added. "Everyone gets three wishes."

The girl smacked the wizards lightly on their heads. "Wishes my ass, aside from whatever it is you actually need me to do. Velasquez, is that you? What's the situation?"

The lead agent approached her. He was suited up in armor and a helmet and carrying his rifle and wrist-tank, which made him hard to identify at first glance.

"It's me. Thanks for coming. Did these guys explain the overall situation to you?"

She nodded. "Yeah. They told me what you guys have done so far, what we're up against, et cetera. I only need to know exactly what you want me to do in order to, uh, find this mysterious thing that's supposedly anchoring the crones in place."

Velasquez elaborated. "Our best guess thus far is that the hypothetical target object is at the center of the horde. Makes sense that something that important to them would be guarded by the bulk of them, though Roland tells me it could also be stuffed into a nook or cranny in a completely different dimension where no one would think to look for it. But we need to take out as many of these things as we can regardless, so the idea is a direct incursion."

"Fun," Bailey quipped. "I assume you want me out in front."

Park walked up. "Of course, but first, let's discuss a little something we can do with an explosive charge..."

CHAPTER EIGHT

Fenris stepped out of the snow and into the portal. Worlds and energies rushed past him as his foot came down on the gritty soil of another plane, the realm of the frost trolls left far behind.

He had not been here for a long time. It was a bleak domain, with parched rust-colored dust and sand and rock over irregular terrain. Huge monolithic boulders were strewn about the landscape, many carved by the wind—or hands and conscious intent, in some cases—into weird, fantastical shapes. Caves opened into the depths of the earth from rises in the land. The only vegetation was an assortment of snaky vines with thorns the size of a human hand.

The sky was a dark slate color, seemingly too close to the ground, and the scanty light that filtered through the thick clouds added to the paradoxical sense of oppression. The land was open, yet the low, dim sky made the place claustrophobic.

Alone, Fenris walked with a casual, deliberate gait. He

had no particular destination in mind. He knew that he'd been sighted moments after he'd appeared and that he was being watched and stalked as he moved.

Good.

Shadowy forms occasionally appeared out of the corners of his eyes as his pursuers changed positions or scampered out of easy sight. He came to a higher patch of land, where oddly-shaped stones were arranged in a rough circle, and a tall, twisted, petrified tree grew at the center.

No sooner had the wolf-god stepped into the circle than he was surrounded. Without fear, he turned to examine his ambushers.

They were lithe, compact humanoids with grayish-purple skin and hair that was the color of pale ashes. Most of them wore it long and tied up or back. The pupils, irises, and scleras of their eyes were all a solid glossy black. Most held bows loaded with barbed arrows, and all wore curved swords at their sides.

Dark elves, another species Asgard had banished to the far fringes of the universe.

"Fenris!" their apparent leader called in a voice that hissed while also being curiously musical. He had a scar down one emaciated cheek. "We know who you are, but not why you've come. You are not welcome, but let us hear your reasons before we decide what must be done."

The wolf-father regarded the elves with a steady, neutral gaze. "Have you been paying no attention to the worlds beyond your own? If you had, then you would know that the beginnings of Ragnarök are upon us. I would speak to your king on these matters if he deigns to receive me."

The creatures conferred in soft whispers. After a moment, the lieutenant of the warband replied, "So be it. We will take you to him, but whether he decides to grant you an audience will be his own decision. Any treacherous acts you might attempt will be met with the wrath of the entire realm."

Fenris bowed his head. "I understand. I will attempt nothing untoward."

The elves, maintaining a circle around him, led the wolf-god across the wasteland, and then down into an especially large cavern. At first they passed through mere tunnels, but soon they came to an area like a subterranean city, with carved stairs and pillars set with black, amber, and purple gemstones. Other elves, civilians in rags or courtiers in fine robes, milled about.

In a grand hall at the rear of the sunken metropolis stood a throne of black crystal. Armored guards with pikes closed in, peering suspiciously at the newcomer as the dark elves' king descended from his seat.

His name was Gormyr, as Fenris recalled. He was taller than most of the others but just as lean and cruel-looking, and his white hair fell in a banded cascade to his waist. He wore elaborate armor of two materials colored like gold and bronze, accented with orbs and bands of obsidian.

"Fenris," the monarch intoned in a voice deeper than that of the lieutenant and thick with sardonic coldness. "What could *possibly* bring you here?"

The deity smiled grimly. "The end of Asgard's rule."

Silence fell over the hall as Gormyr stared at the eyes under the hood. "Oh?" The king sneered. "So you've come to negotiate the surrender of the Æsir and Vanir to us. We shall consider treating you mercifully."

"Not quite," Fenris replied. "Rather, I've come to inform you of how, if you will work according to the plans I've laid, you may participate in the gods' fall. I've already convinced the frost trolls to join me. Whatever your opinion of their intelligence, you cannot deny that they are useful in situations where brute force is required."

He could tell that he had seized Gormyr's curiosity. The king dismissed the warband and brought Fenris closer to his throne, and the two of them spoke in relative privacy at the side of the great hall.

Fenris told him everything that had transpired thus far, and also of his plans involving Bailey. He mentioned the importance of deploying her in unimportant theaters of combat to increase her strength while also keeping her in the dark as to the ultimate agenda.

For the dark elves' part, they needed only to make assaults on the barrier zone between their realm and that of the divinities. The idea was to distract the pantheon, to convince them that the minor skirmishes happening now were an important threat so that their brief "victory" would lull them into complacency right before the final hammer stroke fell upon their heads.

Gormyr's black eyes were soon shining with malicious excitement, and the king began drumming his fingers on the hilt of his sword. "Although we have no specific *reason* to trust you, the opportunity you present is not something we are willing to pass up."

"Of course," Fenris said.

Gormyr went on, "Therefore, we shall agree to aid you

with your plot, so long as you do nothing to convince us that it is a poor idea. I am profoundly unsurprised that you intend to rule in Asgard's stead, but the universe could do no worse than it does at present under the current gods. Do not betray us or disappoint us, Fenris, or you will find us an enemy worse than any you've encountered. Keep to your bargain, and you will discover that we are excellent people to have as friends."

The wolf-father reached out and clasped forearms with the elves' monarch. "I am pleased to hear that," he remarked.

Park said through the communications device, "Fire in the hole!"

Everyone ducked, covering their ears and opening their mouths per the agents' instructions as the explosive charge went off, collapsing the wall of rock that separated the central path out of the valley from the right-hand one. There was a juncture between the pathways beyond the wall, so collapsing it gave them more space to work with while only having to defend the same area from an incursion from the crones.

Bailey wondered why they couldn't simply have her destroy it, but Park seemed set on blowing something up.

Alternately, it could have been because they didn't want Bailey's attention divided between too many places at once since around a hundred of the phantoms had massed beyond the energy barrier created by the poles.

The werewitch dashed ahead, saving the central pole

from the avalanche of smoking rubble and tossing it back toward the agents as the howling specters converged on her. Behind her, she faintly heard Roland tell some of the witches who were new to this, "You folks ain't seen nothing yet."

Bailey filled the entire sky and air in front of her with flames. It was as though a forest fire had begun on that one spot, or a huge bomb had gone off and somehow exploded in a wall-shaped line instead of an expanding sphere. She blocked the heat from radiating back in her direction, thus protecting the others from it, and pushed the sheet of deadly fire forward to engulf the ghost-crones.

They shrieked, their semi-substantial bodies burning and their incorporeal elements partially disrupted by the intensity of the blaze. The flames died out as they moved, but more than half of the creatures were destroyed or at least badly incapacitated, and the rest were in retreat.

"Holy mother of shit!" someone exclaimed.

The agents and witches swept in to mop up the bedraggled remainder of the ghosts while Bailey shielded them from stray attacks.

As the agents vacuumed up the arcane essences left behind, the goddess used telekinesis to clear the mass of rubble created by the explosion, much of which was now glowing a dull red from the heat of the fire-wall she'd conjured. She tossed the hot stones over the mountaintops to the sides and cooled the passage down with a shower of cold rain.

The mortals advanced over the steaming rock. Bailey was out in front, knowing the crones would attack again soon. In the rear, two of Velasquez's men held a pair of the silver poles, seeking to further expand the size of their safe zone.

About halfway to the canyon, the remainder of the first group of phantoms turned around and attacked again. This time they floated in high and tried to bear down on the mortals from above. Bailey conjured a veritable forest of lightning bolts that struck every last one of them. Most vaporized, and those that survived were stunned into immobility. The agents finished them off with the green beams of their disruptor rifles.

Park laughed. "We're on a roll. Everyone stay tight, though. Once we come out of this passage and into the main canyon, things are gonna get ugly, fast."

As they neared the end of the crevasse, Bailey instantly saw why. Roland had told her what to expect. And she'd seen a lot of strange, frightening shit in her short life. But somehow, nothing could have prepared her for what lay ahead.

Like a patch of collapsed wood near the foundation of an old house where termites had formed a colony, the big ragged gorge swarmed with hideous specters, hundreds if not a thousand of them. Her brain needed a moment to fully comprehend what she was looking at.

"Hey!" she called over her shoulder. "Can I just nuke the center of the canyon and be done with it?"

Velasquez's voice replied with, "Negative. We can't risk damaging the target object before we know what we're dealing with if indeed it's there."

Roland confirmed this. "Sorry, dear. I'll make it up to you with a really nice engagement ring, I promise."

"Might want to throw in a six-pack of beer on the side," she suggested, still staring at the canyon.

From a distance, the vast space had looked like a single pit, but as they drew closer, it became clear that it was an irregular area of different shelves of rock that crisscrossed the walls, random and labyrinthine.

They paused, and the agents conferred on tactics. They now realized that the terrain was rougher than expected, so they'd have a tough time getting in deeper. It also meant they could more easily claim and defend territory.

Velasquez waved to the men in back. "All right, put those poles at the edge of the passage. If we get lucky, we might be able to carve off a quarter of this goddamn canyon and add it to our safe zone, but for now, we have the whole pathway under control."

He turned to Bailey. "There's more coming up. Do your thing."

She raised her arms, and a tsunami of water rose a hundred feet high in front of her, the colossal wave crashing down the rambling steps of the inner canyon to engulf the leading wave of crone-ghosts. The deluge spread itself thin only a fifth of the way into the canyon, but by then, it had done its damage.

"Ooh!" Dante exclaimed, "everything's wet. Stand back, folks."

He tossed a single small bolt of lightning onto the slick rocks ahead.

Sparks and steam rose as electricity crackled down through the gorge, wreaking further havoc on the struggling phantoms. Bailey and Roland maintained powerful deflective shields as the agents moved in to neutralize what resistance remained.

Other specters began to filter out around them from small caves and crevasses that hadn't been visible from higher up. The auxiliary witches were pressed into battle again, and streams of elemental magic, arcanoplasm, and glowing shields filled the air.

Bailey turned back and forth, her mind racing as she balanced the needs of helping her comrades against the harrying strikes from the sides and the need to stave off the next wave of the advancing horde.

"Hey," she shouted. "All you guys, focus on getting rid of these fuckers." She flapped her hand to indicate the crones that had ambushed them. "I'll keep the ones up ahead busy."

Two hundred or more were advancing up the jagged slopes. From a distance, they resembled a weedy brown field writhing unnaturally, and the werewitch's spine went cold as their awful screeches wafted toward her on the stuffy air.

Confident that her allies could handle the battle going on behind and to the sides of her, Bailey decided to try something more precise than a single big blast.

She extended her arm and channeled plasma into a continuous stream of short bolts like firing a machine gun, and sprayed the projectiles into the advancing ranks of the crones. Magenta flames rose to the sky as the creatures ignited or disintegrated under the onslaught, but for every dozen that perished, another dozen advanced.

"Clear!" Park's voice yelled. A quick glance assured

Bailey that they were finished dealing with the other phantoms.

She decided it would stop the rest of the horde from advancing at the same time as she neutralized the ones at the front. Breathing deeply as she quickly visualized the next spell, she threw out her hands.

A sheet of ice several hundred feet tall and the width of the canyon materialized in front of the undead legion. Dozens upon dozens of the clone-spirits were trapped in the frozen water, and the ones behind them were blocked from attacking. The ice wall was so massive that the light in the canyon went about three shades darker.

"Nice!" Deanna complimented her.

Bailey nodded. "Thanks."

Velasquez directed his men to approach the ice wall and use their rifles to carve out and destroy the crones nearest the front surface, asking Bailey to keep an eye out in case the whole thing started to collapse. To prevent that, she plugged the holes their weapons made with more ice and surrounded the frozen barrier with sub-zero air.

"Okay," the senior agent announced, "we made a *lot* of progress, so break and recoup."

His men brought up more of the field-generation poles and positioned them so the arcane barrier coincided with the edge of the ice wall. The mortals now had control over their entire end of the canyon, as well as the paths back to the valley where they'd first portaled in.

Velasquez grinned. "And," he gloated, "we took out, what, a *hundred* of them? And by 'we' I mostly mean Bailey, yeah, but everyone has done a great job. Well done."

They rested, and those who were hungry again dug into

the MREs again. Once it seemed safe to assume they'd purchased some breathing room and were in no immediate danger of further attack, Velasquez and Park pulled out folding tablets and asked all present to pay attention.

"Okay," Park began, "while we were waiting for Bailey to show up, Velasquez and I sent Roland's and Dante's suggestions back to the eggheads, and they sent us back a program that coincides with what we're looking for. I think. I'm new at this, sue me."

Velasquez picked up where his partner left off. "This software, in conjunction with the tracking tech we already have, picks up major concentrations of arcane energy that *aren't* tied to living things. So, if we scan the surrounding area of this region of the Other..."

He turned the screen to them, and it displayed a crude terrain map that they recognized as the canyon with many dots of magical presences in front of them, representing the remainder of the witch-ghosts on the other side of the ice. But also...

"We can see that well outside this gorge, there are *other* blobs of light that look totally different. Big, pulsating auras that don't seem anything like these low-level appari-tions we've been fighting, and they're not moving. If we're looking for inanimate objects, those might be it."

Roland, Dante, and the other witches agreed that making for the nearest such point on the map should be their next objective.

"And, you know," Dante added, "it must have taken Callie weeks or months to create this many clones. We wiped out about a quarter of them in one day. There's no way she'll be able to replenish them at the same rate."

"Right," Park agreed. "And if these mysterious light-blobs are their, uh, horcruxes or whatever, we can move in for the kill and deal with all of them at once."

Velasquez turned to Bailey. "Will you be able to stick around and help us through to the end? Honestly, we might not need you at this point, but life would be easier with you around."

She thought about it.

"Well, Agent, I do have other things I need to deal with which, no offense, are equally important to this. If you really need me, I'll try to come back, but that ice will hold for a long time. If you need to go through it, you've got good witches who can help you with that. Carve a tunnel through and lead the crones into a bottleneck, that sort of thing. Or if you can find a way up and out to investigate those auras, the ice wall will protect you while you do. Keep an eye out for any of the crones that try to float over the top, though. Pretty sure they can do that."

Everyone seemed disappointed at the prospect of her leaving. It occurred to her that she might be failing them in her duty as a goddess.

Then again, gods weren't supposed to do everything for people. Mortals had to solve their own problems to some degree.

She embraced Roland and kissed him goodbye. "Keep being smart," she told him. "And we'll see each other again soon, then we can talk about that engagement ring."

"Absolutely," he agreed. "Take care of yourself."

Waving to everyone, the werewitch re-ascended into the path, feeling as though she should be out of physical sight before she departed. Then she opened a portal to Earth and stepped through.

Bailey was strangely unsurprised to find a familiar face was waiting for her by her pole barn out back. What was surprising, though, was that it was someone she'd never seen outside a certain crystalline hall.

"Coyote," she marveled. "I didn't expect to see you here. Don't take this the wrong way, but usually when a god comes to meet me, that's a bad sign."

The trickster chuckled at this. "How does one define 'bad,' exactly? In any event, I know much of what you've been doing lately, dear girl, and that you're tired. The good news is that I haven't come to drag you into anything too strenuous. Not yet."

She sighed. "I'll take what I can get. So, what's the *bad* news?"

He gave her a half-apologetic smile. "That we, the council, have been long in conference, and Loki is among us. Everything he told you, we know too. The implications are most dire, and you are heavily involved in them."

Her gut clenched. Coyote extended a hand and placed it gently on her arm. "And though it was not much discussed, there is something else I know: that in a way, you love Fenris, even if—correct me if I'm wrong—you know the truth and have finally accepted it."

She had no idea how to respond to his words. In fact, she couldn't respond, because it took all her strength and self-control not to burst into tears.

To take her mind off the awful mess of emotions within her, she focused on business. "We can talk about that later. Why are you here?"

"To oversee the next phase of your training," he stated. "You will soon be called upon to do terribly difficult things. We're with you, as Loki said, and for once, I'd say you can trust him. With our help, you can prevail."

"Okay," Bailey acknowledged, "though if you don't mind, I'd like to take a break. Been busy doing goddess stuff, as you might be aware."

Coyote smiled. "Yes, quite all right. In fact, as long as I'm here on Earth in mortal form, I thought we might have dinner together."

She cocked an eyebrow. "Sounds good. You might want to, uh, look a little more human, though. A third of this town is werewolves, true, so a...half-coyote...were-man...*person* wouldn't attract *that* much attention, maybe, but still."

"So be it." The god shrugged, and in the blink of an eye, his canine features vanished.

In place of the strange yet oddly pleasant-looking humanoid creature he usually appeared as was a fiftyish Native American man in a maroon t-shirt and blue jeans. His face was lined and weathered, yet his eyes twinkled with good humor, and the strands of gray at the temples of his long black hair gave him a distinguished look.

Bailey pursed her lips and bobbed her head. "Yeah, that'll work. I'd say let's go to the diner, but honestly, I was there earlier, so I'm thinking the sandwich shop instead if that's okay with you. They got good cheesesteaks."

Coyote replied, "cheesesteaks are a personal favorite. A guilty pleasure, you might say. Shall we walk or drive?"

Normally she would have preferred to walk, but after fighting a small army of witch specters, she decided to take the truck. During the short drive, she listened with a grave expression as Coyote summed up how the other gods had reacted to Loki's bad news.

"You know," she pointed out, "Loki doesn't have the best reputation for trustworthiness, but he makes a convincing case."

The man beside her concurred but didn't press the issue.

They parked in the lot behind the shop and wandered in. It was a small establishment, with only three tables plus bar space. Two of the tables were full, so Bailey and Coyote went to the bar.

The young woman behind the counter, a freckled redhead, gave Coyote a curious look or two but didn't ask about him. It wasn't uncommon for Bailey to be seen in the company of strangers from out of town.

While waiting for their sandwiches, they sipped their drinks. Bailey's was an orange soda, Coyote's a cola.

"Admittedly," he commented, "I'm not a fan of mainstream sodas. More partial to quirky third party independent or lesser-known brands since they're usually more interesting and could use the support."

"Gotcha," said Bailey. "I'll see if Gunney can round you up one of those sometime. He occasionally picks up weird stuff, but it's usually good."

Seconds after their cheesesteaks arrived, the doors behind them opened, and in strode four young men. Bailey recognized them, not personally or individually, but as a type: vacationers from somewhere closer to the coast, or maybe California. Mixed backgrounds, but they all looked rowdy and cocky. They'd probably been drinking up on one of the mountains before they'd come down into Greenhearth.

"Man," the first guy said, "this place is crowded for being tiny as fuck. It's gonna take forever to get food here."

"Yeah," a second agreed, "out in the boonies, they're not used to people's time being valuable, and they always work really slow."

Bailey frowned, picked up her sandwich, and took one bite.

The quartet approached the counter and began heckling the redhead with a mixture of bizarre menu questions, half-assed flirtation, and condescending aside-remarks delivered as though the entire shop couldn't hear them.

An older couple seated at one of the tables was watching them. The man called, "Hey, now, be polite and wait like everyone else has to. No reason to pressure the girl like that."

The group turned on him and snapped something about stupid rednecks. The hair on Bailey's arms bristled, and she started to stand up.

"Hold," said Coyote, placing a hand over hers. "Sit and enjoy your meal. I'll take care of this."

A shoulder-twitch from one of the oafs, who were facing away from them, told Bailey that he'd heard the Native man's words.

She squinted at Coyote. "I thought you weren't

supposed to, uh, intervene, with, you know, stuff that'll draw attention." Meaning divine magic.

"Don't worry," he assured her. "There are simpler ways."

He came up behind the four vacationers and asked them to please either behave themselves or leave, and one reflexively shoved him. He fell back a step and was suddenly poised in a sidelong position on springy feet, his hands rising toward his face and forming into fists.

"That was a foolish error," he informed them.

The girl watched, dumbfounded, as the god in human form became a blur of motion, the blue of his pants, red of his shirt, and black of his hair streaking through the air of the confined space. Two of the guys lashed out clumsily with their fists but hit nothing.

The Native man's fist slammed into the leader's ear, sending him reeling and clutching the side of his head. By the time the blow had landed, Coyote was spinning around to elbow one of the other guys in the back of the head, and he lurched against the wall.

Bailey took a couple more bites of her sandwich and sipped her orange soda. Thus far, she was impressed.

The third vacationer tried to bring his knee up into Coyote's gut, but the lithe man twisted aside and punched the knee, making the kid gasp in stunned pain and stop to check for injury. At that point, Coyote kicked him in the groin—not hard enough to ruin the rest of his day, but enough to send him to the floor doubled up.

The fourth guy sputtered, "Shit!" and ran, pushing out through the door. The bells attached to it rang cheerfully as he departed.

The first two guys were close behind him, telling him to

wait up. The third, who'd taken the knee and ball shots, tried to get to his feet but was having trouble. Coyote helped him up and told him, "Please remember today's lesson in the importance of courtesy." Then he shoved him out the door after his friends. He hopped along down the sidewalk until he was out of sight.

The counter girl sighed with relief. "Thanks, man, whoever you are. I guess if you're one of Bailey's friends, we can rely on you for stuff like this. I finished making the first two of their sandwiches, though."

Coyote smiled. "I will buy them and save them for later. Or one, if you're allowed to have the other yourself. I'm not sure what this place's policies are on employee meals."

When he sat back down, Bailey let out the laugh she'd been holding in since it became clear who would win the fight. "Beautifully done. Nice restraint, too. I'd have probably sent at least one to the hospital, but you got the job done by ruining their weekend instead of their whole month. Unless the guy who took the elbow to the jaw lost a tooth or something."

"I don't think he did," Coyote mused. "But thank you. I'll try to teach you how it's done since you can always use more instruction in such matters."

She raised her soda cup and tapped it against his. She wished it was glass, but they'd have to make do. "Here's to that."

A little later, they departed the shop, taking the extra sandwich with them and stashing it in Bailey's fridge. Her brothers were out meeting with other Weres, hopefully recruiting them as a reserve force in case the shit hit the fan. She wasn't used to seeing them not be home or at the Elk.

Bailey decided that the old family farm, about two miles away into the countryside, would be the best place for her and Coyote to begin their training. The god offered no objections. The drive was slow and bumpy since the property was only accessible via a crappy dirt road that wound through dense woods.

They talked as she drove. Coyote seemed curious about the town and what it had been like for her growing up, and he cracked silly but amusing jokes after every second or third thing she said. Chortling, she went on to regale him with the capsule version of her life story, pausing to insert little asides about specific things she remembered and was nostalgic about.

She also mentioned the hardships and uncertainties, however—in particular, the anxiety she had lived with for so long about being forced into marriage by the age of twenty-five, as per ancient lycanthrope custom.

Until she'd become an official shaman.

"So yeah," she concluded, "I was spared that fate, thanks to...well, to Fenris."

She was silent for a moment after that.

"It's okay," Coyote told her.

CHAPTER NINE

"Good," said Coyote. "I'm going to try to elbow you in the face. See if you can break my arm at this range."

He and Bailey had been drilling in clinch fighting and grappling skills. They were inches apart, their arms intertwined and within range to knee one another in the groin or stomach. The girl had only the vaguest of idea of how the hell she could break anyone's arm like this unless she released him and opened herself up to a punch, kick, or throw.

She tried three times and failed, then Coyote showed her a subtle technique for readjusting her balance and position so that she could seize his arm and apply pressure to it by using his own movements against him.

The girl gave an appreciative nod. "Nasty, but might be helpful."

"Sadly," the deity commented, "the most efficient sorts of combat are often *brutally* efficient, and it would be better if we didn't need to use them ever. But sometimes we do, and it's better to know how if you must."

Bailey wiped the sweat from her brow. The day was getting hot. "Agreed."

They drilled several more techniques for what felt like hours, if not a day or more, though the sun did not move as much in the sky as she would have expected, and night did not fall.

Most of the fighting style Coyote demonstrated to her was oriented toward speedily disabling one's opponent before they could fight back, or neutralizing their attacks by exploiting the openings they created. Elbows, knees, breaks, chokeholds, and the like were emphasized. It reminded her of what little she'd seen of advanced military close combat.

They separated after Bailey seemed to have the hang of an oblique knee-strike to the kidney that led directly into throwing her adversary over the same knee.

Coyote smiled in a grim way. "All right. You have done well so far, and I think your abilities have seen a slight improvement in this short time. Let's take a break and drink some water."

She had no complaints. They chugged from a gallon bottle and sat on the grass, admiring the thick clouds that wafted through the bright blue sky.

Bailey had been under the impression that hand-to-hand combat took many hours to gain basic competence, let alone mastery, and she mentioned as much to her trainer. "Although I'm a fast learner, most of the time," she added.

"Generally true," Coyote acceded, "but in this case, I have been sneakily aiding you this whole time in a way you don't seem to have been aware of."

She looked at him sidelong. "Is that so? May I ask what the hell you mean?" She was baffled; either he was referring to a minor thing he'd been doing for a long time, or he meant a trick he'd deployed during their sparring session that was too subtle for her to have grasped.

The man chuckled, looking pleased with himself. "Certainly. You will recall that I am a trickster, and part of being a trickster-god is knowing how to weave illusions. Not only things like astral doubles of oneself, but the ability to create minor perceptual hallucinations."

"So," she mused, "does that mean you've been tinkering with my senses? If so, I kinda wish you would've told me."

He spread his hands, looking innocent. "I'm telling you now, aren't I? But yes. I have been altering your perception of time. You may not have noticed, but we've only been practicing for a few hours. Your brain has interpreted it as being much longer. As such, the impact and efficacy of the practice we've gone through are enhanced. You've learned more, and more quickly."

She blinked. "Weird, but it makes sense. Next time, warn me, okay?"

He pouted. "Knowing about it decreases the effect, but fine. Fair enough."

He leaned back on his elbows and looked at the sky. She joined him, saying nothing for a time.

While they rested, Bailey thought of something.

"Coyote," she said, "I haven't seen Fenris for a while—over a day at least. I'm not sure what he's getting up to. Have you guys been keeping tabs on him? If I go looking for him or call him without a legitimate reason, he might suspect that I'm on to him, since the whole time I've known him, he's disappeared whenever he feels like it, to do…whatever it is he does."

The trickster god craned his neck and looked up at the clouds. "We have some knowledge of his movements and a fairly good idea of what he's up to, yes. Fenris is devious, but he's not as clever as he thinks he is, nor is he as clever as I am. It's part of my portfolio as a deity, after all."

"True," the girl acknowledged.

Coyote went on, "Our council discussed these matters at great length. We are working on ways to deal with the situation and ensure that Fenris does not succeed. You, Bailey, are a key element of *our* plans, just as you are the linchpin of *his*."

She grimaced as she stared into the distance, trying not to reflect too deeply on the extent to which she was someone else's tool either way.

But it also meant that she had the power to tip the scales. No one had told her she had to simply stand back and hope for the best or any such crap.

"And," Coyote added, "given that, I would say we have a good chance. You have risen to the challenges you've faced so far, have you not?"

She nodded. "Yeah. I have."

They spend another minute or two feeling the summer air of evening around them, unspeaking. Bailey found she had another question, one which had been lurking in the back of her mind ever since she'd mostly accepted that Loki was right about her longtime mentor.

"Coyote. I don't understand why is Fenris doing this? What's he trying to accomplish by destroying Asgard and bringing about the goddamn end of the world as we know it?"

The man shook his head, his salt-and-pepper hair wafting in the breeze.

"I cannot fathom his reasoning. Perhaps vengeance for his having been excluded from the council, perhaps a misguided belief that it will somehow improve the universe. Or perhaps he's simply abandoned himself to the prophecy that states that he *must* act as the catalyst for Ragnarök. There is no *sane* reason, but then again, the gods are not required to be sane. Some of us have existed forever—or near enough to forever to make no difference to you—and they are the way they are, that is all."

Bailey skimmed back over conversations she'd had with Fenris, searching for things he'd said that might act as clues to his agenda. It was difficult to find much that stood out, and besides, how much of what he'd told her was true?

Coyote added, "Other deities, perhaps, started out as beings of sense and balance, but the long, slow, brutal procession of time has driven them insane. I don't claim to know what the case is with our acquaintance, the wolf-father, but whatever his reasons, he must be stopped. Too much catastrophe will befall the world—multiple worlds, in fact—for us to allow it to happen."

Rubbing her eye, the girl sighed, "Yeah, I can agree with that much. Are we training any more today?"

"We are," the god confirmed. "Allow me to show you more magic that may be of use to you in the struggles to come."

Though she was tired, Bailey recognized the gravity and necessity of their situation and complied.

Coyote showed her advanced tactics for manipulating the earth and ground, a mixture of geology and mysticism that exceeded anything she'd thought of or been trained in thus far.

Back and forth, the two drilled the spells and motions. She created small shifts in the earth hundreds of feet below them, and they watched as tiny earthquakes began, or the lay of the terrain began to shift.

"Furthermore," Coyote added, "it is also possible to use the earth as a source of strength and vitality. You can draw upon its power. In a way, it's like when you grounded yourself before bleeding out Aradia and Freya, as Fenris showed you. This is the reverse, you might say."

Following his instructions, she sent out astral tendrils with her mind and locked into the ground around her. Bailey felt its living force: the reserves of kinetic, heat, and electromagnetic energy stored within its materials, as well as the potential for life in its fertile, plant-friendly soils or deposits of insects, worms, and other small creatures.

"I feel it," she announced. "It's like it was always there, but I never took notice of it."

Coyote smiled. "Good. Yes, there's tremendous power stored in obvious places, places so obvious you wouldn't think to look. As a shaman, this is part of your heritage and your mantle. Shamans have always been tied to the elements around them and the latent magical strength of the planet."

The werewitch felt another vista opening within her, a new skill or set of knowledge she could use.

She hoped that when the time came, it would be enough.

Bailey had felt like driving her Camaro, though it was only a few minutes into town. It was late morning of the day after her training session with Coyote, and having slept long and soundly following her workout, she felt like traveling in style.

En route to the auto shop on the slope off the main road, Sheriff Browne noticed her and waved to her, adding a stern glare to remind her to keep her speed at a reasonable level. She waved back and drove exactly thirty-one miles per hour in the thirty zone.

Shortly after the sheriff's station, she turned onto the side road that took her to Gunney's shop. When she arrived and climbed out of the vehicle, she saw the repair bays empty, and the aging mechanic sitting on a lawn chair near the rear of the structure. None of the other employees were present.

"Damn," she muttered under her breath, "must be a slow week."

Gunney waved to her. "Hi, there. Hope you weren't looking to get some extra hours in on the side since we're customerless at the moment."

"Nah," she retorted, "just wanted to hang out and see how you were doing."

He stood up. "That works. Want something to eat? I got subs. Turkey club in this case, for a change of pace."

She stretched her back muscles. "Sure, sounds good. I had a cheesesteak yesterday anyway."

They brought out the sandwiches and ate them with orange soda. Gunney had picked up a whole case of the beverage, so the werewitch didn't complain about him drinking one of "her" oranges.

While having their early lunch, Bailey filled the old man in on all that had happened, noting the way his eyes grew wide and distant.

He slowly shook his head in befuddled amazement. "Shit," he muttered. "You're not making all this stuff up, are you? I'm joking. I've seen too much with my own eyes, though I can't say I've been to this parallel dimension or whatever it is. But it sounds like what you've been doing, if you kinda sum it all up, is stopping problems before they happen so things can be peaceful. Am I right?"

The girl sipped the last of her soda. "More or less."

"Well," Gunney went on, "I don't have any cars for us to work on, so if you're in search of a task that will put your mind at ease, all I can think of is sweeping the damn floor."

"That works," she said.

They each grabbed a broom and began clearing the shop floor of dust, grime, and small bits of random debris, pushing it out into the gravel lot out back. While they worked, the mechanic talked.

"Granted," he began, "not having any customers is on the boring side, but it's also nice to relax. I know it won't last. There'll be more work to do soon, and when I get back to it, I'll have to neglect other things— the tasks that all have to be done in order to win that day off, like today. We can't always be at peace. Sometimes we've got to fight through bullshit for quiet times to happen."

She swept a small pile of dirt out the back door and stood for a minute, leaning on her broom. "True enough."

Gunney came up beside her. "I'd say that's where you're

at, too. You've got a lot on your plate, but trust yourself, your family, and your friends—all the people who've worked with you and helped you so far. Well, except you-know-who, but let's not get into that. Otherwise, you have what you need to get the job done. I know you can handle it. Then there will be peace again."

The pair looked each other in the eyes without speaking until the older man broke the silence.

"For once," Gunney remarked, "I think we should take a ride, only it's my turn to drive. What do you say?"

"Sure," she replied at once. "But where to? And what wheels we taking?"

The mechanic smiled. "Up the mountains to the east, I'm thinking, up to that scenic overlook. You know the one. As for the wheels, well, I was saving it for a surprise. Check this out, girl." He stood up and beckoned for her to follow him out back.

She bit her tongue to keep from asking, but mumbled to herself, "This oughta be good."

Gunney had a way of acquiring new and interesting vehicles seemingly out of nowhere. Then again, it could also be one of the obscure projects he'd been gradually working on for years. There was so much shit in his scrapyard out back that despite the many years she'd known him, she didn't have a firm mental inventory of it all.

There was nothing in the gravel lot immediately behind the shop. They headed instead to the fenced-off yard. As it grew closer, Bailey could see a particular car at the center of a clear patch of ground. It was an antique, and bright cherry red.

She gave a whistle. "Damn, Gunney. That thing's nice. A Cobra?"

"This," the mechanic explained, "is a '65 Shelby Cobra. Or AC Cobra, which is what they called it in the UK since it was first made over there. Renamed the 'Shelby' when it was sold in the U.S. of A. Ford V8 engine, not something you see every day. I've been working on it more or less in secret for, oh," he breathed out, "nine years or so."

She gawked at the thing. "Those two white racing stripes up the front are a nice touch," she observed. "I'll probably burn in hell for saying this, but it kinda reminds me of an Edsel, only not shitty."

"An Edsel?" Gunney gasped, paling in horror. He swallowed and took a moment to get himself under control, his eyes going distant as he dismissed the last half-minute from his mind, suppressing all memory of it ever having happened.

"Now," he went on, as though she hadn't made that remark, though she had to chew a lip to keep from laughing, "since today is its debut again, I'll drive. You can ride shotgun. Let's go."

She climbed in, noting how old-fashioned and attention-grabbing the thing was while still being classy. It wasn't her usual "type" of car, but Gunney was obviously thrilled with his handiwork.

He fired up the engine, then stopped the car out front while he quickly locked up the shop before hopping back in and piloting it out onto Main Street. Once they'd reached the edge of the town, his foot turned to lead.

He chuckled. "Sit back, and let me show you what this old man can do."

Bailey grinned evilly as the speedometer climbed past eighty, Gunney maintaining his speed in spite of the increasing curvature and elevation of the road. He was forced to drop to "only" seventy once they were in the mountains, but she had to admit he was handling the vehicle with tremendous skill all the same.

What he was doing was also dangerous as hell, and the fact that she recognized it seemed strange to her.

Not too long ago, she, as a reckless post-adolescent, wouldn't have cared. She'd just have enjoyed the thrill of it. At present, her mind seemed to have grown up since she was calculating all the things that could go wrong.

It made no sense since her past self would have been doomed if anything had gone wrong, whereas these days, she as a goddess could avert catastrophe with a flick of her hand.

Still, she enjoyed the ride, and so did Gunney. They traded jokes, encouragement, and off-color remarks as the eastern Cascades zipped past, the cliff wall to their side growing shorter as the gorge grew deeper. Finally the Cobra sped onto the scenic lookout picnic area in a faint cloud of bluish smoke.

"Well, shit," Gunney panted, "that was about the most fun I've had since, well, the time you and Roland and me raced up here a week or two ago, however long it was. But aside from *that*, it's the most fun I've had in years."

She smiled and hugged him. "Hell of a ride," she concurred.

They spent a quiet half-hour together, looking out over the hazy peaks and green woods, before climbing back into the antique sports car and driving back home. This time, the mechanic went slower.

He offered to drop her off at her family's house, so she had to remind him that her car was still at his shop.

"Oh, right." He grunted. "Slipped my mind. I guess I am getting old, after all."

"Not *too* old," Bailey reassured him.

They climbed out of the car after Gunney had locked it up in a lean-to shed in the far corner of the scrapyard. Before Bailey departed, the older man took her in a tight embrace.

"Bailey," he said softly, "I'm proud of you, girl. You probably know that, but it bears repeating."

She rested her cheek against his hat. "I do, but yeah. Thanks. It's nice to hear."

"Go do what has to be done. And kick some ass. Like you always do."

He gave her a final pat on the back, then watched as she walked away, climbed into her Camaro, and made ready to drive it the short way home.

Near dusk, Bailey decided she'd rested enough, and there were people who needed her help.

She breathed in. "All right, Roland, hope you and your witch buddies from Seattle and those damn government guys knew what you were doing this whole time." She supposed that if they'd truly needed her, they would have found a way to call for help or sent someone through a portal.

Or something. Anything. She refused to consider the prospect that bad shit could've gone down so fast that none of them had had time to reach out to her.

Having been in the portion of the Other where they'd attacked the army of witch-specters, Bailey found it fairly easy to locate it with her mind and open a portal of her own to it. She pictured the mouth of the tunnels that led into the cliffs and down into the main canyon, which, last she'd seen, the agents had established as part of their turf.

A purple gateway opened before her, and she stepped through. Cold; dizziness; then it melted and she stood on red rock in a desolate landscape of tall crags and dark violet skies.

She bumped into Agent Park. "Whoa!" he exclaimed. "Nice to see you again, but still. Careful."

"Yeah, yeah," she retorted, taking in the scene before her. "Sorry."

Most of the ice wall she'd conjured still stood, but there were two holes or tunnels in it, near each wall of the canyon. Probably made by the mortal forces for excursions deeper into enemy territory.

For the moment, everyone was resting, though they looked tired and bedraggled. She must have caught them shortly after a battle.

Roland pushed his way through the ranks of men and women. "There you are. How long has it been back on Earth, anyway?"

"Uh," she replied, hugging him, "a full day, maybe a bit more. I had a slight perceptual illusion yesterday, so that threw me off slightly. Don't ask. Fill me in on how things've been going in here."

He did. As she would have guessed, the human forces had made the holes in the ice and launched a couple more attacks against the horde of ghost-crones, eliminating another hundred or so of them and pushing their lines farther back.

Park explained, "We had some of the boys from HQ portal in to bring us more of those poles, so our perimeter extends past the ice wall about a hundred feet in a semi-circle from the mouths of those two tunnels."

Velasquez had trotted over by now. "We've made progress, but it's going to take a big push to reach the nearest of those light-pulses on our scanner screens. Based on what we can see, there should be a slope or path on that side of the canyon," he gestured with his chin, "leading up to the first one on that plateau beyond. Your help would be immensely appreciated, Bailey."

She put her hands on her hips. "Hey, what are friends for?"

The force spent another five minutes preparing, mentally and materially, for battle, then took their positions as Bailey, Roland, and the lead agents conferred on strategy.

"Me out in front," Bailey said immediately. "Right? Roland should be near the front also since he and I are experienced in fighting together, and he's damn good with a shield. I imagine you'll want your guys close behind me."

"Yes," Velasquez confirmed.

Everyone took their positions near the ice tunnel farther from where Bailey had portaled in. On their scanners, this corresponded to the top of the screen, so they arbitrarily referred to it as "north" even though the Other wasn't likely to have magnetic poles the way a planet did.

At the head of the column, Bailey strode through the tunnel, noting the eerie silence within the thick ice. Up ahead, she could see the faint purplish field created by the barrier poles, and beyond it, the horde.

They emerged into a small area crammed against the reddish rock of the canyon wall. Otherwise, they were surrounded by eldritch crones pushing futilely on the arcane wall, then retreating in pain and fear or hovering a hand's breadth before it and moaning and howling at the mortals.

Bailey glanced over her shoulder at her allies. "Get ready."

Moving her head toward the mass of enemies, she raised her hands. A rippling series of explosions of fire and plasma began right on the other side of the poles' barrier and streaked onwards into the rest of the canyon, blasting and consuming witch-spirits as it went.

Velasquez barked, "Move!" and everyone surged forward, while Bailey used another round of freezing rain to cool the smoking rock. Behind her, agents vacuumed up the remaining phantom essences while Roland handled shields and the other casters tossed offensive spells at the retreating horde.

The squad pushed forward, annihilating at least a hundred of the crones. Soon they reached a portion of the canyon wall to their left that had collapsed in a rockslide, forming a crude ramp or staircase onto the plateau to the "north."

Bailey moved past it, then, remembering the earth

magic Coyote had taught her, cut the canyon in half by manipulating entire shelves of stone, walling off the portion controlled by the specters from that controlled by the mortals.

"Fuck, yeah!" Park gloated. "Nice work."

Bailey smiled. "Thanks."

Having again increased their territory, agents moved the poles forward to claim and protect the extra space. Everyone briefly rested to prepare themselves for the next phase of the operation.

Bailey also smoothed out the jumble of rocks on the upward path, making it less treacherous and more like an uphill road. It was harder than she'd thought it would be, but she managed. The difficulty made her wonder if constructive and transformative magic was harder than destruction.

Velasquez waved his hand and the human force jogged up the path, Bailey once more on point.

On the plateau beyond, they encountered only random stragglers—pockets of six, eight, or ten crones at a time, which they easily destroyed. As they neared the point of light the agents' screens had shown, they encountered a mass of phantoms about fifty strong.

"Positions!" the lead agent shouted.

Not wanting to accidentally damage the mysterious power source they sought, Bailey surrounded the crones with a spiraling vortex of lightning and frozen acid shards, with enough gaps between the elements for some of the specters to try to slip through.

A smattering of individuals succeeded, but most were caught in the barrage and ripped apart. The few that made it past were quickly vaporized and contained by the Agency's weapons.

Roland let out a deep breath. "Well, we're undefeated so far. Let's see if our luck holds out now that we've found...this, whatever it is."

Bailey dismissed the deadly cyclone, and they all moved forward.

The object was in sight. The agents confirmed that it was the pulsating nexus of arcane energy their scanners had turned up, and since the crones had seemingly been defending it, Bailey had no doubt that they'd acquired their target.

"Man," one of the guys behind her remarked, "that is just *weird*."

She had to agree.

The thing was partially sunken into a shallow depression in the earth like a miniature crater, yet it reached higher into the air than the tallest man in the group—seven feet or so. It was as big around as a large tree, but it did not resemble one in any other way.

At first, Bailey wondered if it was a living thing. It was a bulbous mass of pulsating nodes connected by thick, sticky tendrils and a heavy gelatinous substance. The thing was black in certain places and clear in others, mainly in the centers of the nodes, though those glowed with blue light. It made an odd humming sound that rose and fell as though it were breathing.

Roland came up beside her. "I don't think it's a creature, exactly. My guess is that it's the arcane equivalent of a mineral deposit, only it's 'animated,' you might say, by a large amount of magical essence. So, more like a machine, really—inanimate matter that moves around because it's charged with energy."

"I see," Bailey mused. She could sense a strong aura of occult force emanating from it.

Agent Velasquez joined them. "Is it acting as the anchor for these things like we theorized? The scanners are picking up a ton of signals coming off it."

"Probably," said Dante, who'd been standing five or six paces aside from them. "I don't see what else it could be. We've stumbled upon a dumping ground for coalesced magical potential." He smirked. "Let's destroy it and see what happens."

Velasquez arched an eyebrow. "You sure about that? I'm all for it if you guys are confident it will dissipate the crones. What we *don't* want, of course, it to be caught in a nuclear blast or to get possessed by unleashed spirits or something fun like that."

They agreed that everyone would stand at a safe distance, that Roland and a handful of other witches would maintain a powerful shield, and that Bailey, aided by Dante, Charlene, and the agents' disruptor rifles, would destroy the pulsating mass.

Bailey reminded her lover, "Don't worry about making a hole in the shield for me; I can summon shit on the other side of it. If that doesn't do the trick, and if there isn't a big kaboom, you can make holes for the agents to fire through."

"Roger," said Roland.

Once the thick wall of translucent light protected them, Bailey took a deep breath and unleashed hell.

The sky opened up, and a column of white light

consisting of concentrated heat, electromagnetic energy, and arcanoplasm descended on the slimy blue-black thing. It was briefly silhouetted within the destructive radiance before it dissolved and flew apart in spattering pieces.

Dante, Charlene, and the others joined in by flinging bolts of lightning and sheets of flame at dispersed chunks, which were blown apart or burned with ease.

There was no obvious blowback. However, Bailey did feel an odd, nauseating sensation as the power stored within the bolus vaporized, and a faint blue light lingered in the air where it had been.

Then they heard it: wailing cries in the distance like wind through trees, rising in a crescendo and rapidly fading.

"It's them," Deanna surmised. "They're dying without this thing to anchor their strength."

The bulk of the spectral horde was too far away to see much, but it did look to Bailey like some of them were vanishing and the mass was growing smaller.

"Hah!" Roland laughed. "It would appear we were correct. However, I think we only affected some of them. There have to be more of these things, and possibly something bigger controlling the entire horde. At the very least, we'll need to dispose of the remainder of these lovely spore-blob-trees or whatever they are to neutralize Callie's army."

A brief discussion followed, though its only conclusion was that Roland was probably right.

"All right," said Velasquez, speaking to his men as well as the witches, "let's make camp. We move against the next one as soon as we've rested and recharged."

CHAPTER TEN

They'd destroyed the third of the spore-anchors and were taking a meal break when a tall dark-amethyst portal opened in the center of the camp.

Bailey sat up straight, instantly alert, as Fenris stepped out of the doorway. Everyone stared at him, but the wolf-god paid no heed to anyone but Bailey.

Looking at her from under his hood, he stated, "I need you again."

She frowned. "Is it urgent? I'm helping these guys take care of this army of witch specters. We've wiped out two hundred or so, and we're less than half of the way through the damn things. They're going to invade the Northwest if we don't deal with them soon."

Fenris glanced around, taking in the situation in the span of two or three heartbeats.

"Yes," he replied, "it's urgent. What you have here is a matter of some concern, but your friends should be able to handle such weak manifestations with their combined skills and weaponry. I need you to oppose another and different incursion, one which will require a goddess."

Behind him, a couple of the greener agents grumbled in protest at having their heavy artillery taken away, but Velasquez stepped in and informed them who their new guest was.

Fenris clearly heard this exchange but ignored it.

Sighing, Bailey got to her feet. "Okay. I'll come with you. Tell me about it on the way in. One condition, though. As soon as the worst of it is dealt with, I will come back here to finish aiding these guys."

The hooded figure nodded. "Agreed. But come with me now. We don't have time to waste." He stepped aside from the portal, giving her a clear path into it.

The werewitch looked at Roland, whose face was drawn with concern. "Don't worry," she told him, "you guys will be okay. And I'll be back soon."

With that, she walked into the purple gateway, and everything vanished around her.

They stepped out into a portion of the Other she was familiar with: the endless dismal swampy area of gnarled trees, spongy ground, black ponds, and curling mists. She looked at Fenris. "Is the threat here, or is this just our stopping-off point?"

"The latter," he answered her. "We will need privacy while I brief you on the nature of the mission before we plunge in."

She swallowed and inhaled. Not only did the god's task sound like it was going to be dangerous, but she found herself speculating whether Fenris knew she'd spent a day with Coyote while he was away. Training to fight *him*, if need be.

"Bailey," the wolf-father began, putting a hand on her shoulder, "Asgard, and by extension, the mortal realms, are again threatened by an invasion from one of the dark peripheral worlds and the beings who live there. In this case, the dark elves, who are perhaps more dangerous than the frost trolls were."

She squinted. "Dark elves? Never heard of those, aside from in fantasy games and shit."

"They are in the Norse legends associated with our pantheon," he extrapolated. "I have reliable information that they are massing near the borderland between their world and that of the divine. If they succeed in breaching the barrier, as with the trolls, they will overthrow the gods and very likely move on to conquering and destroying Earth. We cannot allow that to happen."

The girl tightened the muscles along her jaw. "If that's true, then yeah, we'll need to do something about it."

Though his eyes were hidden beneath his hood, she felt Fenris looking at her pointedly. "Why would it not be true?" he asked.

She felt a flicker of panic—had he finally begun to suspect her?—but suppressed it. "You said you had reliable information, but it sounds like you haven't seen it with your own eyes yet, so there's a chance it could be bullshit."

He smiled. "You're savvy as well as powerful. Yes, there is a chance, but I doubt it."

She was relieved that he seemed to believe her, but she remained concerned about the mission.

"The dark elves sensed Asgard's vulnerability the same way the trolls did," Fenris went on. "They are not to be taken lightly. Although smaller than trolls and lacking their great strength, they are deadly opponents—experts in swordsmanship and archery, with a savage and cruel streak. Also, they are skilled in certain dark and twisted magicks that have gone centuries or millennia unpracticed by much of the universe. Spells you may not have encountered. This will be no easy fight, Bailey, but difficult is not the same thing as impossible. We can prevail over them, and we will."

She nodded with a barely perceptible motion. "Yeah. I kinda thought I'd seen enough 'dark and twisted magic,' though. Not gonna lie, I'm nervous about what the hell else these guys might have."

"We shall see," Fenris intoned. "Now, prepare yourself."

He closed his eyes, chanted in a low voice, and spread his hands to open another portal. This time, he stepped through first. Bailey hesitated for an instant, then followed him into the familiar disorienting coldness of astral travel.

She emerged close behind the wolf-god in another landscape that was just as desolate as the canyonlands where the crones had gathered but unique.

"Where are we?" she inquired. "A different part of the Other, or a whole different world?"

Fenris adjusted his hood. "Another world entirely. A tumor that grew from Asgard, you might say."

For some reason, his phrasing it that way bothered her immensely.

The land before them was dim and windswept, the landscape consisting mostly of rusty stone and gravel interspersed with weird twisted vines, petrified trees, and immense boulders eroded into bizarre shapes. Dark clouds hung close overhead.

It was quiet. Nothing moved or made a sound except the dry, chilly breeze.

She turned to the deity. "Are you sure this is the right place? It looks abandoned."

He set off at a steady pace, apparently having picked a direction at random. "I am sure," he responded as she followed him. "And it is not abandoned, it's meant to *seem* that way."

They continued through the dim wasteland, encountering no one, only a procession of boulders and the occasional cave mouth. Bailey wondered if they should investigate the caves, but for the time being, she had no choice but to trust Fenris's judgment.

"Hey," she said to him in a low whisper. Although they appeared to be alone, something about the eerie silence of the place made it seem unwise to speak too loudly. "I haven't noticed a damn thing. No offense, but either your informant didn't know what he was talking about, or I'm missing something, and we're walking right into a trap."

The wolf-god slowed his pace a tad to focus on speaking to her. "Rely on your shifter abilities, not your human perceptions or witch-magic, or even your abilities as a goddess. It is important that you don't lose touch with the skills you possess as a wolf in humanoid form."

That made sense. Bailey shifted into wolf form, keeping herself the same size to preserve her clothing, and followed Fenris on all fours, pricking up her sensitive ears.

As they trekked on, still there was nothing. She shot her companion a confused look.

He tapped his nose.

Feeling foolish, Bailey ignored the lack of information coming to her via sight or hearing. Instead, she sniffed the air and realized at once how careless she'd been.

The scents of many bodies wafted on the breeze. It was subtle since their smell almost blended with that of the realm, but it was there. It shifted as the creatures moved around. Many were following the pair, and others were upwind, or off to the sides, probably watching.

Fenris, she said with her mind, *I can smell them now. A couple dozen or more.*

He smiled. *Good. And yes, that is my conclusion also. This world of theirs is cold, harsh, and antiseptic. Virtually nothing lives here, which means that the dark elves, who are among the few creatures who do manage to survive, can easily be smelled, given the lack of interference from other biological organisms.*

They moved toward a circle of stones, and Bailey noticed the smells growing stronger. More of the beings —dark elves or whatever they were—were gathered nearby.

The creatures who live here, Fenris went on, *mostly exist underground. They have superb darkvision and have learned over the eons to move in near-total silence or to disguise their movements as the natural shifting of sediment or the noises of the wind, but nothing can fool the nose of a wolf.*

It was true, and briefly, the girl swelled with pride—pride, and a sense of camaraderie with the man, or god, who'd trained her and been with her through so much.

But...

There was no time for Bailey to contemplate the thought any further. Two dozen dark, lithe shapes leaped out at them as if from nowhere at all. Curved blades of metal the color of charcoal were in their hands.

Shit, the werewitch mentally cursed, and she pounced on one in midair. She crashed into the elf, knocking him aside, and her teeth ripped out his throat before his sword could find its way between her ribs. Then she was in motion again.

Before the next clash, she got a better look at their assailants, who were slender humanoids with skin of deep ash-purple and silvery hair. Their ears were long and pointed, their eyes dark and malevolent. The ones charging her held black scimitars, which they whipped about with impressive speed and control.

Worse, though, a third of them had hung back to launch barbed arrows from black bows. Bailey bowled into the nearest swordsman and shoved him between her and an archer taking aim. Vicious satisfaction rose in her chest as the arrow penetrated the elf's chest and he slumped to the ground.

Fenris had shifted into his lupine form, much larger than hers, and stomped a swordsman to death before charging the bowmen. Three black arrows protruded from his shoulders, but he seemed not to notice them.

Bailey was confident he could handle himself. She conjured a pair of shields around the sides of her body to protect it from arrows and blades alike, then pounced on a pair of elven fighters. The shield on her left side bowled one over, and her jaws sank into the lower leg of the other. Before he could bring his scimitar to bear on her head or neck, she stepped on his sword-arm and crushed his skull with her jaws.

The battle proceeded for another minute or so. Bailey had to agree that the dark elves were vicious fighters, but ultimately they were no match for a pair of werewolf-deities. Twenty of them lay dead or dying, and the remaining four were in full retreat.

As the girl prepared to celebrate, she noticed more dark forms emerging from the desert—many more. A hundred at minimum.

Fenris's psychic message came loud and clear, echoing her own thoughts. *Run.*

The pair bounded away from the elves, who had formed a kind of moving crescent with the bulk directly behind them, but several closing in from the sides to flank them and cut off their flight. Fenris knocked aside any elves who came too close, and Bailey launched a couple of quick, flying attacks to slash and batter any archers who tried to shoot them.

They stayed ahead of most of the attackers, but they couldn't run forever.

Fenris shifted back into human form in the blink of an eye and looked over his shoulder. "There!" he barked, indicating a yawning black cave mouth. He hurled a struggling elf into the air to crash into a boulder, then dashed toward the opening.

Bailey was at his side in an instant, back on two legs herself, willing her clothes to repair the minor damage they'd taken. "Is it safe in there? If anything comes up from behind us while we're still dealing with these guys…"

"It's our only chance," the wolf-father growled, and he hurled an exploding fireball into the faces of three elves charging him. They sprawled, burning and dead, in different directions. Other warriors jumped over their corpses to attack.

The girl conjured an ice wall, smaller than the one she'd made in the canyon of the crones but no less sturdy, which blocked the majority of the elves off from the cave. A few of them were able to work their way around the edges single-file, and she and Fenris made short work of them.

After they'd killed another four, the elves hesitated. Bailey could half-hear their whispered conversation, though their strange, hissing language was unknown to her.

Fenris, meanwhile, was inspecting the dark tunnel behind them. Its interior was oddly smooth, and it sloped downward out of sight. There was no evidence either for or against the prospect of further attacks from that direction.

"Bailey," the wolf-god began, "I suspect this cave may lead to the elves' inner sanctum. There, I might be able to speak with their leader, King Gormyr, and reason with him, or at least trick him into a parlay until we can plan our next move."

She blinked. "Okay, that could work since you managed a truce with the trolls' king, and he was probably a lot dumber than theirs is. What do I do? Come with you, or hold this passage?"

She thought she could see the shadows of more elves about to sneak into the narrow passage between the ice and the rock, but it was hard to be sure.

Fenris shook his head. "No need." He raised a hand and the ice wall grew, extending at the ends to seal the cave's mouth from the outside world. The elves had no way to get to them unless they gradually hacked through the frozen mass or knew of a back passage that intersected the tunnel.

Bailey let her breath out. "Good deal, but that won't hold forever. They seemed pretty determined to kill us."

"Yes, they ferociously defend their territory from any and all outsiders, but your work here is done. We've killed enough of the dark elves to make them wary of us and set an example of what will happen if Gormyr does not come to terms. I believe I can handle it from here on, and I'd say you could use a break."

He swiped a hand, and the cave was bathed in soft purple light as a portal opened before him. "This," he pointed out, "leads back to your home in Greenhearth. You'd best get some rest and refresh yourself before you gallop back into that canyon to assist your friends. They'll likely be fine without you for a time."

Bailey wondered if she could trust Fenris to deal with the situation, given all that he seemed to be guilty of. Then again, the elves had seen him kill their people. There was no way they could be collaborating on anything.

"Okay," she said, moving toward the shimmering gateway. "Call me if you need me, but I can't promise I won't be busy. So much shit going on in the universe lately."

Fenris took his first steps down into the tunnel. "There is," he agreed.

King Gormyr regarded Fenris with his usual expression of hostile and arrogant disdain, mingled with a sly curiosity.

"Thus," the wolf-god elaborated, "Bailey demonstrated

that she has the necessary prowess. Since we were forced to slay several of your warriors in order to maintain the ruse, I assume the ones you sent were among the weaker and more incompetent, so we did not cull anyone of great importance."

"Yes," Gormyr confirmed, fingering the pommel of his sword. "She managed to triumph over my lesser fighters, but what assurance have I that she'd be a match for the greatest of them?"

Fenris smiled. "They did not pose much of a problem. Bailey would have had to work harder to kill the stronger ones, but her failure was extremely unlikely. Meaning no offense to their prowess, but she is a goddess, after all."

The elven king rubbed his smooth chin. "You speak sense, though I'd rather have her duel one of my master swordsmen to be sure. Still, you are confident that she can take your place during the opening salvo of Ragnarök?"

"I am," Fenris stated, standing at his full height, his jaw firmly set. "It will be a pity to lose the girl, and yet, as a mortal, she was destined to die regardless. Likely a dull and common death until I gave her the opportunity to sacrifice herself for something far greater, namely, the liberation of our universe from the rule of the Asgardian pantheon."

Gormyr's eyes narrowed and seemed to look far beyond the face of his new partner. "Far more lives than hers have been sacrificed toward that goal across countless centuries. We have waited so long for this opportunity. Do not disappoint us, Fenris."

"I shall not."

Fenris walked an acceptable one pace behind the king's elbow as the two ambled across the throne room toward the corridor that led to the dining hall. They were soon to attend a feast.

The wolf-god spoke as they moved. "If all goes according to plan, I will survive the beginning of the End, and with my accumulated knowledge and experience of the workings of Asgard and the council with its two non-Asgardian deities, then, with my help, you shall triumph. The barriers that separate the divine realm from yours will fall, and the exiled peoples, the beasts, and the monsters of the universe shall have their revenge. You may plunder and destroy to your hearts' content."

Gormyr let out a dry chuckle. "Such a splendid offer. I am tempted to refuse simply because it sounds too good to be true."

"It *will* be true," Fenris insisted. "And when Asgard has fallen, you and your allies may move on to seek new territory in other realms, within the few and reasonable restrictions I will suggest. A new age is dawning, and we will rule it."

They came to the dining hall, a vaulted black chamber with a long table and chairs of polished stone and crystal. It was lit by flaming braziers, though the elves could see well enough that it was scarcely necessary. Mostly a formality.

The king sat at the table's head, Fenris at his right hand, with the elves' chamberlains and top warriors and generals rounding out the other high-ranking positions. Various lieutenants and middle-manager types occupied the far end. Everyone rose briefly for the king, then re-seated themselves, waiting in silence until the first course was brought, at which point Gormyr would be expected to speak.

For the moment, everyone tended to their private conversations, and Fenris spoke again to the monarch while the dark-elf aristocracy listened intently.

"Soon," rumbled the wolf-god, "I will speak to Jormungandr, the World Serpent. Though a simple and irrational creature, it is not immune to intelligent offers. More importantly, it may be the only creature powerful enough to destroy Thor once the battle begins. If I succeed, we will have nothing to fear from the warrior son of Odin."

"Good," Gormyr replied. "We do not *fear* him, but the sooner he is disposed of, the more quickly we can turn to ravaging his allies and relatives."

A bevy of slaves appeared with the first course of the feast, the roasted meat of a large subterranean reptile creature, along with boiled mushrooms and a reddish-black wine made from strange berries that grew beneath the surface of the rust-colored domain.

Once the table was full, King Gormyr stood with flagon in hand and proposed a toast—to their coming struggle, and to Fenris the Wolf-Father, who had proposed the plan and would lead them to victory. The other diners raised their glasses in turn and cheered, a savage note in their dry voices.

One of the king's generals looked at Fenris. "You have our support, renegade son of Asgard. See to your end of this bargain, and we will continue to support you until the end of time."

"Good," said Fenris. Addressing the entire chamber, he added, "The time will soon be nigh to join with the frost trolls. Thanks to my efforts, you will find them amenable to our mutual cause. Whatever past differences you had with them are of no relevance now, for the army that shall overthrow the gods is rising to strike."

Again, they cheered.

CHAPTER ELEVEN

Bailey sat alone at her usual table in the diner half of the Bristling Elk. They had a special going on, two ham and cheese sliders for the price of one, so she'd bought four, along with a side salad for fiber and a glass of orange juice. She felt like she'd been eating too much junk lately and could stand more vitamins and plant matter.

Not that she'd put on any weight, given how much exercise she'd been getting.

Around the corner near the front entrance, she heard the doors open and heavy footsteps came in. One of the waitresses up there gasped audibly.

Crap, Bailey thought, chewing and swallowing the food in her mouth as quickly as she could. Somehow my wolf-sense or whatever is tingling to indicate trouble. Might be those city assholes Coyote beat up, might be some of Roland's fan club looking for him. Who knows?

But as the newcomer rounded the corner into the dining area, she saw that she was wrong.

It was Balder. He wasn't wearing his golden armor or

other divine accouterments, of course, having traded them in for a nice button-down cream-colored shirt and well-pressed slacks. Otherwise, though, he'd done nothing to tone down his appearance.

As such, Tomi was following him with a sort of rapturous expression, her mouth slack. Bailey was afraid she might drool on the floor. She'd always gotten the impression that Tomi preferred men who were a little rough around the edges, hence her obvious lust for the Nordin boys, but Balder was so blindingly attractive in his male-model way that it didn't seem to matter. His long golden hair sparkled even in the low lighting.

"Oh," Tomi gasped, "uh, sir, just, um, sit wherever you want! I'll be along to take your order in a second." She glared at the other waitress on duty, who was also gazing at their new customer as if hypnotized.

To Bailey's total lack of surprise, he came over and sat across from her. The fact that he was here meant he must have something important to share, but she wished he could have waited until she was done eating. Now she'd have to put up with Tomi's shenanigans through the whole rest of her meal.

"Hello," the god of beauty and innocence greeted her. "Are you well?"

"Yeah," she returned. "Fine, mostly. Busy as heck lately, trying to save multiple worlds while keeping abreast of all the godly political crap going down. How about yourself?"

He smiled pleasantly. "Oh, I'm good. Thank you for asking."

Tomi rushed up and took his order, complimenting him on his shirt and cracking jokes the whole while as he grinned at her in a bemused but confident fashion. The werewitch wondered if he fully understood the effect he was having on the poor woman. He seemed aware that *something* was going on, but being an immortal, he might not have grasped quite *what*.

Balder ordered a club sandwich, heavy on the bacon, along with a root beer.

"Ohh, that sounds good!" Tomi cooed. "How do you want your bacon done?"

"Crispy, please," replied Balder.

The waitress rushed off to place the order, shooting two backward glances at the god as she left.

Bailey sipped her orange juice. "I had a club yesterday; it was from the sandwich shop, though, instead of the diner. Slight difference. Also, it's weird to me that you're a bacon fan."

Balder smiled. "Food of the gods, if you ask me," he quipped.

It took the girl a second to realize he'd made a joke since it hadn't occurred to her that he had a sense of humor. "Oh, ha-ha, right. Most of us mortals—I'm not one anymore, but close enough—are fond of it also. Except for people whose religion forbids pork or are concerned about cardiac arrest. It's so damn tasty, though."

"Indeed," the deity agreed. "So, Bailey, do you know why I'm here?"

Tomi reappeared with a tall glass of root beer, and he thanked her with a warm smile that made her shudder. Bailey was afraid she would stick around, but one of her other tables started giving her the eye, forcing the woman to tend to them.

The werewitch looked into her visitor's big blue eyes. "I'm guessing you've come for the same reason Coyote did: to teach me more stuff and offer training and advice, right?"

"Indeed. You would benefit from learning more of the ways of swordplay and combat magic, and I can instruct you in them better than anyone. People sometimes think I am too nice to be a warrior, but they are mistaken."

Bailey didn't doubt it. The first time she'd met Balder, he'd summoned a swarm of Viking ghosts to attack her and Roland as a test, and not long ago, she'd faced him in single combat. With a sword and shield in hand, he was nothing to fuck around with.

The girl nodded and bit into her last slider.

Balder asked her to quickly review what Coyote had taught her so there were no redundancies since they didn't have time to repeat things she already knew. She told him, and he seemed satisfied.

After his sandwich arrived, he spent a couple minutes eating, a look of deep satisfaction on his face as he chewed the crispy bacon and washed it down with soda. Tomi lingered for a minute to stare at him and sigh before assuring him that anything he needed from her—anything at all—would be his if he requested it. He thanked her and said his food and drink seemed fine.

Bailey cleared her throat. "That may not be what she meant, but let's not get into that. Anyway, could you elaborate on what you'll be showing me?"

"Of course." He set down his half-eaten club. "En route to enacting his ultimate plans, whatever they are, Fenris will be coming for us, the Asgardian pantheon, which means that I am among his targets, so I'm afraid it's personal. I would prefer not to die. Training you in weapons-based fighting that you might be able to use to defeat him will be both beneficial and cathartic."

The girl wiped her lips with her napkin. "Makes sense."

"Quite honestly," Balder continued, "I cannot stand Fenris, and it has been thus for eons. He is humorless, cynical, and dishonest, though we've only just come to realize *how* dishonest. However, I am not certain I could overcome him in combat, but Tyr may be able to, and on the side, I can train you to help. Do you agree to that, Bailey Nordin?"

She breathed in through her nose, pushing all feelings out of her head. "I do."

"Damn," Bailey said and whistled. "How much did you pay for this thing?"

Balder shrugged. "I'm only renting it. Please, hop in."

It was an electric-blue 2020 Porsche 911, one of the nicer sports cars she'd seen outside of Gunney's collection of antiques. She was all too happy to climb into the passenger's seat and secretly hoped he planned to drive a nice long way.

They went southwest out of town, speed climbing toward a hundred miles per hour as Greenhearth fell away behind them and they climbed the little-traversed mountain roads. Past the point, Bailey recalled, where Roland and the rest of the town had confronted the Venatori Inquisitor who had tried to place the whole community under lockdown. The road had been badly torn up, but it was repaired by now.

"Holy shit," the girl exclaimed as Balder continued his mad exercise in reckless driving. Yet his control was perfect, and he reflexively made every necessary adjustment to keep the car in its lane despite the winding and steep quality of the asphalt path before them.

The drive ended five minutes later at a remote scenic outlook, the one where the Weres of the Hearth Valley had held a memorial service for several of their own who had fallen against the Venatori. Normally it was a touristy place, though not heavily visited. At the moment, it was empty.

"Ah, good," remarked Balder. "We'll have privacy. I'll set an enchantment to ensure it stays that way."

They climbed out of the car and strode to the center of the paved area atop the low peak, with other mountains and vales spread out in all directions around them.

Balder pulled a medieval European longsword out of thin air and tossed it to the girl, who managed to catch it only at the last second in her surprise. She looked it over; it was a classic weapon of its type: cruciform, approximately four feet long, with a two-handed grip and a relatively narrow blade that would be good both for cutting and thrusting attacks.

"Nice," she remarked. "For whatever reason, I assumed we'd be using, you know, Viking swords."

The god of innocence tittered at that. "The iconic sword type associated with my original worshipers is my favorite for sentimental reasons," he conceded, "but I am skilled with all forms of blades, and you ought to be as well. The fourteenth-century longsword is a well-rounded weapon and an excellent place to start. However, I shall oppose you with something a bit different…"

He put a hand behind his back and pulled out a long, elegant rapier. The curled and upswept guard upon the hilt and narrow blade made the type of sword unmistakable, but somehow Bailey had thought of rapiers as being smaller, bendier weapons, like modern fencing swords. The earlier and more martially-oriented blade Balder wielded was a thick, deadly, forty-inch spike mounted on a one-handed grip.

"Bailey," he began, "it is time you learned true and proper swordsmanship, above and beyond what you practiced in the training grounds not long ago."

That rankled her. "I did fine then. A sword is a sword, isn't it? You swing the edge toward someone as fast as you can, then you stick them with the pointy end or however that quote goes; you know the one I mean. Besides, I can turn into a wolf and call in a magical airstrike whenever I need one. Honestly, isn't this kinda redundant?"

He laughed again, and there was a faint note of contempt and condescension in it. "Not at all. In the many realms of our universe, there are many magical weapons, and knowing how to wield something similar will serve you well. Trust me."

With that, he attacked.

She'd expected him to give her a brief introduction before they got to it, but she'd also learned to expect the unexpected from supernatural beings. Fortunately, Balder began with simple alternating thrusts, high and then low, which were fast enough to have been deadly if she'd been caught unawares. Since she was paying attention, they were easy to parry.

Still, Balder forced her back step by step, his offense coming too quick for her to counterattack. Particularly as her sword, while less heavy than she'd expected, was not as nimble as his.

Then he stopped. "Not bad," he opined. "You have good instincts for the flow of a fight and were able to block my strikes, which, by the way, were legitimate attacks, albeit simple ones. Had you slipped up, the blade would be lodged in your face or chest."

She nodded. "I imagine we don't have time to train the *safe* way."

"Indeed. Anyhow, your footwork is rather sloppy. You managed to remain balanced, an indicator of your general aptitude for combat. However, greater smoothness and precision is needed for proper high-level swordplay. Allow me to show you..."

He drilled her in the complex footwork associated with multiple different types of fencing and European martial arts. There wasn't time for her to attain full mastery, of course, but with all the techniques she'd learned for expanding her mind and retaining information, it was nonetheless educational. More than anything, she tried to focus on the underlying philosophy of moving her body in tandem with her sword, supporting herself on her feet at all times, and positioning herself in ways to gain leverage and minor tactical advantages over her opponent.

Then they again locked blades, with Balder employing different kinds of attacks, showing her various ways to strike and block, and urging her to combine those with the footwork lessons, blending everything into a harmonious, nearly mechanistic whole.

Whatever enchantment the god of beauty had used to keep people away, it must have worked. No one bothered them as the sun began to sink behind the mountains. They continued, never breaking to rest for more than two or three minutes at a time, as the sky went dark and the stars became visible.

Not until the sun reappeared over the distant peaks to the east did Balder conclude the lesson. Bailey, huffing and increasingly stressed, had been forced to call upon her extra reserves of strength as a shifter, not to mention taking heart to Coyote's previous lessons about drawing vitality from the earth.

The girl leaned on her sword and stared down at the valley. All she wanted at the moment was a glass of water, followed by a soft bed.

"Good," Balder congratulated her. "If you can remember all you've learned, I would say you possess a serviceable grasp of the basics. Wielding a sword, you will not simply commit inadvertent suicide."

"Thanks," she gasped. "Good to know."

He gave her ten minutes to sit down and drink some water.

"But," he added, "that was only our first lesson. There is another, though it ought not take as long as the first."

The girl scowled. She had little choice about participating, but she wanted to protest. Dragging the process out would leave her too exhausted to remember all she'd learned.

Balder then showed her how to imbue a sword with

magic. He enchanted his rapier so flames spewed from the blade and left saffron streaks in the air as it moved. Then he summoned a bolt of lightning to strike it, so it sparked and made white flashes when it struck things, especially her sword. She had to focus hard to repel the electricity from entering her body and stunning or even killing her.

"To do this," he explained, "you must first focus your will and attention on the sword, imagining the structure of its steel as a foundation on which to build or a nexus around which the magical energy will revolve. Try it first with fire, then with lightning."

Sighing and clearing her mind of fatigue and distractions, she summoned a flame, but at first succeeded only in heating the blade to dull redness. It started to bend out of shape, and Balder had to magically repair it twice.

On her third try, she succeeded, but the flames persisted for only a minute. It took eight tries before she could maintain the fiery blade for a good three minutes, which Balder considered adequate.

"Well done," he complimented her. "Now, lightning."

This time she not only damaged the sword but electrocuted herself and had to use magic to heal the superficial damage and pain-shock the lightning caused. Balder frowned but restored the sword, advised her on how to better control the electricity, and watched as she tried again.

Seven attempts and she had an electrified blade under control for about two and a half minutes.

Balder nodded. "That will do. You are far from a master, but you are no longer a clumsy novice, either. With some, it might have taken over a week. You have done it in a day. Be proud. However, the time has come to give me back my sword."

He smiled and extended his hand.

Though it was a nice enough weapon, Bailey was happy to be rid of it. "By all means, take the damn thing," she grumbled.

The blond god took the blade, and it vanished the moment it touched his hand. Then he twirled his hand behind his back and produced another, different sword.

Bailey blinked, staring at the training weapon's replacement.

It too was basically a European longsword, though slightly shorter and broader of blade, about three and a half feet. Curiously, it had no crossguard, only blade, handle, and pommel. It looked as though it were made of shining quicksilver and glowed with a bright iridescence that reflected the sunlight like a rainbow in a mirror.

"It's beautiful," she whispered. "Is it—"

"Special, yes," Balder finished for her. "Magical, certainly. At my request, and according to my specifications, it was crafted by the dwarves, who are masters of metalworking and possess certain magicks of their own in addition to the powers I lent them for the task. It has one purpose: *to kill a god.*"

Something deep within her went cold with a strange mixture of fear, anguish, and borderline religious awe. She accepted the weapon. Nothing happened when she touched it, but it felt perfect in her hands that even were it not enchanted, she'd have realized that it was a priceless piece of superlative craftsmanship.

Balder went on, "I am trusting you with such a potent

artifact because we, the other deities, are all on Fenris's hit list. He *expects* us to have such weapons, and having taken me out, it would fall into his hands to use against other gods. He will not anticipate it being in *your* possession. Hold onto it, Bailey, and keep in mind that it can only kill a weakened god, not one at full power, so do not rely upon it at first. Save it for when the fight is about to come to an end, then end it."

She stared at the blade as the meaning of Balder's words sank in.

"Farewell," he added, then turned around. When Bailey looked up, he was gone. So was the Porsche.

Fenris strolled across a lush green landscape, more oak savannah than forest since much of it consisted of rolling plains of emerald grass. The trees were regularly interspersed amidst the terrain, though hardly dense. The sky, mostly clear with wisps of white cloud, was visible overhead, and there were boulders—many great heaps and chunks of ancient limestone.

The lycanthropic deity kept walking until he came to a pile of rocks the size of a modest one-story human house. Something about it was subtly different from the boulders he'd come to previously. He stood before it and waited.

In the span of two heartbeats, the rocks moved and rose, rolling up over each other to assemble themselves into a humanoid shape of stones linked by unseen forces. The head-rock, with vague depressions that resembled eyes and a mouth, turned toward the hooded man.

"What," it asked in a voice like crumbling sediment, "are you doing here?"

Fenris raised a hand, palm outwards. "I come in peace," he stated. "And I wish to speak to your leader. Will he receive me?"

The rock giant made a rumbling sound as its component parts ground against each other in thought. "If you are true to your word, perhaps he shall. Come, and make no foolish errors. We will not tolerate treachery."

"Of course."

Fenris followed the giant up a gentle slope toward a ring of hills where the trees were larger and the scattered rocks more numerous. They reached a rough wall of many different types of stone, within which was a courtyard of quartz and gypsum.

At the center of the courtyard grew a massive tree, as big around as a tower. A recess had been carved into its trunk and was lined with flat stones in the shape of a strangely majestic throne. There sat another rock giant, larger by a head than the one Fenris had followed.

To the sides, piles of minerals assembled themselves into the attendants and bodyguards of the king, who turned his face-boulder toward his guest.

The monarch's voice resembled a small earthquake. "You are Fenris, yes?"

"I am," responded the wolf-father. "Perhaps you have been paying attention to what's been happening lately, perhaps not. Either way, I would inform you of it, and of the role you can play in bringing about Ragnarök and overthrowing the gods of the Asgardian pantheon."

The king of the giants stared at him for a long moment, then said, "Go on."

He told them of all that had happened with the frost trolls and the dark elves and of his plans involving Bailey. With her as the catalyst, the prophecy could be fulfilled, but in such a way that he would endure to lead the renegade peoples in a usurpation of the divine authority. They, the rock giants, would share in the coming victory alongside their allies, with only minimal obeisance to, and supervision from, him.

Creaking and grinding sounds filled the courtyard as the beings of stone contemplated the god's offer. It seemed at least five minutes before their monarch gave his answer.

"We accept your proposal, Fenris," he began. "We have spent too long banished to this dull and peaceful realm, which the deities thought would cool our tempers. We love battle and relish the opportunity to crush. It is part of who we are, and in our prison-realm, we have no enemies to fight. What better foes than the very gods who exiled us? Lead, and lead well, wolf-father, and we shall follow."

Slowly, Fenris's lips rose at the corners in the shadow of a smile. "Good. Since I've planned this whole matter in great detail, you will experience no disappointment in my leadership. For the moment, I need you to marshal your forces to attack the boundary zone between your realm and that of the pantheon. Draw their attention; frighten them and convince them chaos is descending upon the universe of its own accord. Let them panic *before* the real strike befalls them."

Once more, the giant rumbled, "This we can do."

"Excellent." Fenris raised his hand again in a gesture of

thanks. "You will hear more from me soon. Good luck, my friends."

Since Balder had teleported his Porsche with him when he'd departed, Bailey walked back to town, or occasionally jumped into the air and flew when she thought no one was looking, surrounding herself with a cloaking shield to be safe. Random travelers passing through the valley would see no more than a distorted shimmer in the sky.

It wasn't only her being airborne that she wanted to hide, it was also that she was carrying an extremely powerful magic sword.

As she descended to the street and rounded the curve leading to her house, she bumped into Roland.

"*Oof*, sorry," he quipped, acting more flustered than he was in truth. "I screwed up the portal coordinates a tad and ended up in *front* of your house rather than behind as usual."

Before she could say anything, his arms were around her, drawing her to him. He gave her a short but deep kiss and nuzzled his forehead against hers.

"Thanks," she breathed, "I needed that. Was up all night fencing with Balder."

Roland cocked an eyebrow. "Is that what they're calling it these days? Ugh, I'm going to be thirty in a little over a year. Can't keep up with the dirty slang forever."

She slapped him, and he exaggerated the impact. "Dork," she said. "Anyway, you used up your one bullshit joke for the day, so no 'is that a sword in your pocket, or are you just happy to see me?' lines."

He spread his hands. "If you say so. Where *did* you get that? Balder, I assume?"

"Yeah." She glanced around, listened, and sniffed the air. "Listen, this thing is important. I'll tell you later, but I need to get it hidden somewhere before anyone sees me with it."

Nodding, he stayed by her side as they went into the house, then down into the basement, where they wrapped the sword in an old blanket and placed it beneath a couple of boxes of ancient magazines and random knick-knacks.

She wondered if it might be better to keep it on her person, but next time she saw Fenris, how would she explain it? She didn't think that he'd fail to notice its awesome presence, whether or not she tried to disguise it with an invisibility enchantment.

With the blade hidden, the couple reascended the stairs and sat down at the dining room table. Her brothers were home and waved to them from the living room. Although it would seem to outsiders as if they never worked, they ran a successful furniture-building business from the house, so they were almost always home. Their clients, few and far between because their pieces were expensive, came to them.

"Wait," Kurt began, "who are you people again?"

Jacob threw a pillow at his face. "We're glad you're both back safe. Good news, also; most of the Weres in the area are with us if any shit goes down. I think they're getting tired of all this danger and weirdness, but they're loyal and tough. We can count on most of them if we need them."

"And," added Russell, "you know you can count on us. To the death."

She nodded. "Shouldn't come to that, Russ, but thanks, guys. I mean it."

Bailey and Roland filled the brothers in on the gist of what had happened, then they headed out to the pole barn, where Roland's makeshift bedroom still lay, to be alone.

"Shit," Bailey muttered, "this must be what it's like for those couples where one person is a high-powered executive who works sixty hours a week and the other is active-duty military or something. Don't have a 'relationship' so much as conjugal visits every once in a while."

The wizard barked with laughter. "I don't know why," he chortled, "but that's *really* funny. Probably because it's true, more or less. But the crew back in the Other is doing okay for the moment, so I'm glad we have the opportunity for a conjugal visit. Finally."

She put her hand on his knee while he stroked her hair. "I hope," Bailey mused, "they're rotating the witches and agents back to Earth to take breaks. Seems like they were doing fine at holding the perimeter. How many of those disgusting blob things are left?"

"Not sure," he reported, "but we took out two more of them. There are another two that the Agency tech has found so far, but there might be more scattered gods-know-where. We're making progress, anyway."

She closed her eyes. "Good. If I ever have the chance to spend more time with you guys in there without you-know-who dragging me off to fight random assholes, I'd say we can wrap this up and be done with Callie and her crone army once and for all."

Roland grinned. "I am very much looking forward to that. After this shit, she has it coming to a greater extent than she did as a mortal witch, which is saying something."

Bailey stretched her legs. "Yeah. It's not over yet, though. I need some damn sleep, but once I'm refreshed, we'll kick her ass. Well, all of her."

The wizard laughed again and sighed. "In a way, it's good that things have come to a head like this. And no, that's not another dirty joke. I mean, we've had the upper hand during this whole fight against the eldritch specter-things, so we know we can win, and then we can deal with Fenris. We beat a god before, and we can do it again. Once that's done, there won't be anything else. Peace. Only peace."

"I hope so," Bailey said softly.

"I know so." Roland moved around to rub her shoulders. "We can live a normal life together. Well, as normal as is possible with me dating a goddess, but I can finally get you a proper ring, anyway."

She chuckled and rubbed his hand. "Thank you." The weight of her extensive efforts was bearing down on her, she realized. She wasn't in her usual feisty mood to trade verbal barbs. Roland seemed to grasp this and was content to simply relax alongside her.

After perhaps half an hour, the wizard suggested, "Want to take a short walk outside? I know you're tired, but nothing refreshes like the woods. I've grown to appreciate that now that I've gone native in this microscopic hamlet."

"Sure," she agreed. They strolled outside, surprised to discover that the afternoon was waning into evening. Time seemed to be passing more quickly.

The girl decided her lover was right; the fresh air did her good. Still, she soon found herself wanting to head back and collapse.

"Let's go to bed early," she offered. "I think we both need it."

He pinched her ass. "Right."

Slapping his hand away, she growled, "To *sleep*. In the morning, if no one interrupts us like usual, we'll see."

He made a pouty face but only said, "Deal."

CHAPTER TWELVE

The Agency came to their door at eleven the next morning.

Jacob, sighing, answered it. "Oh, hi. You guys again. Guessing you want to talk to Bailey. She's upstairs."

The girl heard the exchange from her bed, where they'd retreated after the walk, and she quickly slipped into her clothes and made ready to head down as Roland begrudgingly sat up beside her. After half a minute's freshening up in the upstairs bathroom, she descended the staircase and saw Agents Velasquez and Park waiting for her.

"Hi," she opened. "The usual, or are we doing something different this time?"

Velasquez adjusted his dark glasses. "Both in a manner of speaking. We're going back into the canyon, but frankly, we're getting tired of fucking around. Also, the boys back at HQ have finally realized this is serious. Come out front, if you would."

Roland followed as the werewitch accompanied the agents into the bare area that served as mutual driveway and parking lot for the Nordins as well as their neighbors. It was filled with agents, about fifty total.

"Nice!" the girl commented. "Of course, it's not like I plan to lean on you guys for the dirty work. I'm the goddess here, so I'll do the heaviest of the heavy lifting. Still, it's good to have more backup."

"Right," Park agreed. "And with more men, we won't have to stop to recharge our weapons as frequently since we can rotate waves of troops into and out of battle as needed, keeping continuous pressure on those things."

Roland nodded with an appreciative look. "Your research and development team ought to do something about the charging issue, though. It's nearly as bad as using weapons that require *ammunition*, for fuck's sake."

"Ha-ha," Velasquez replied in a monotone. "If you're ready, let's go. The sooner, the better. These guys are the cream of the Agency's crop, and we can't borrow them indefinitely."

Bailey asked for five minutes to prepare herself. She also made the decision to duck downstairs and grab the sword from under the crates.

Yeah, she told herself, Fenris might pop out of the air again and see it and wonder what it is and where it came from. I can probably tell him that I made it; he thinks I'm smart enough and strong enough that he'd believe that. Probably. And it might be useful against the Callies. If it can kill a weakened god, I'm sure it will massacre a bunch of crone ghosts.

She and Roland said goodbye to her brothers, then reemerged and announced that they were ready to go.

Velasquez stared at the thing in the girl's hands. "The

hell? A *sword?* It doesn't even have a handguard! Magical, I'm guessing."

"Yep," Bailey stated.

Roland took a step toward Velasquez as though preparing to confide in him. "You know, I noticed the lack of a guard myself and thought about saying something. Then I remembered that when it comes to defense, we can make our *own* handguards the size of a giant ice wall."

Velasquez frowned as a couple of his men snickered. "You're hilarious, kid, now go attend to your girlfriend's needs or whatever. We're going in."

Ten minutes later, they all stood on the safe side of Bailey's ice wall within the canyon, near the natural slope that had led them to the first of the gelatinous magic-nodes. Bailey saw that the mortal forces left there to hold the fort numbered less than a dozen. The only witches who'd remained were Dante, his girlfriend Charlene, and three other sorceresses Bailey didn't know personally, and six of the original twelve agents.

Velasquez stepped up. "We sent everyone else back for R&R. Our perimeter's been holding, so we had every reason to surmise that these few could manage while we gathered reinforcements."

Dante waved. "Hey. Good to see we've got the big guns back. And the big sword, from the looks of it. What is that thing? It looks like a longsword, but it doesn't have a guard!"

"Wow," Bailey riposted, "really? I hadn't noticed."

Charlene poked the wizard in the ribs. "I'm sure she can think of a way to protect her hand if she gets in a sword-fight with these things."

"True enough," Dante conceded.

Velasquez waved a hand. "Right, right. Everyone form up. There should be another node in the canyon a short way beyond Bailey's second artificial wall." He gestured at the mass of rock she'd created last time to block the rest of the gorge. "The plan is a full-frontal assault to get to it while we reduce the numbers of the enemy as much as possible."

Bailey took the lead, with Roland and four elite agents immediately behind her. Then she swiped her sword toward the huge wall of stone.

It parted down the middle, the halves slowly swinging inward like a titanic double door. The shelves of sediment and minerals ground against each other and left dust and gravel in the air. Before them, the rest of the canyon opened up, swarming with eldritch crones.

Bailey grinned as the rush of battle came over her. "Here goes nothing."

She charged forward, holding the sword vertically at her side with her right hand while throwing her left forward. A rippling column of fire and plasma streaked through the center of the gorge, incinerating a hundred or so witch-spirits. Then she parted the flames in much the same way as she'd parted the stone, pushing the two walls of blazing death to the sides and burning more of the phantoms while preventing others from attacking them from the flanks.

Velasquez shouted, "Excellent work. Everyone, forward!"

The entire force jogged ahead. Bailey had cleared a good third of a mile for them, and when she'd split the wall of fire in half, she'd pushed all the residual heat along with it. The stone beneath their feet had returned to normal temperature.

Another few hundred of the creatures were streaming toward them from across the canyon, and others had snuck around the sheets of flame to attack from the rear or sides.

The agents and casters in those positions quickly dealt with the stragglers while Bailey plunged into the main force ahead. She threw horizontal tornadoes of lightning and ice, tidal waves of acid and plasma, and huge projectiles of burning metal. Callie's doubles disintegrated by the dozen, yet their numbers meant that the carnage represented only a fraction of the entire force. Bailey watched as a couple dozen floated toward her, close enough for her to have hit them with a thrown softball, howling in their creepy and mournful way.

"Fine," she mumbled. "Say hello to my little friend."

A bolt of both lightning and fire descended from the sky, striking her sword. Though it took a moment of intense effort, she stabilized the enchantment and hoisted the glowing blade over her head, swinging it rapidly but with tight control. She remembered most of Balder's footwork lessons as she carved a swath through the specters.

The blade cut through their ethereal forms as easily as if they were flesh, leaving wounds that burned and sparked. Any crone hit by the weapon dissolved in seconds, leaving only the vague essence for the agents to suck into their wrist-mounted tanks.

Time passed, and the battle raged on. It felt like perhaps half an hour when silence settled over the canyon as the witch-things dispersed. The conflict was not yet won, but

Bailey suspected that they'd wiped out most of the horde. Two or three hundred more hovered overhead or nearby, hissing at them and trying to decide whether to press the attack., and before the mortals was another of the blue-and-black gelatinous sculptures, the anchors for the crones' magical power.

Velasquez pointed. "Neutralize it."

"Roger," said Bailey. She ran up and swung her sword through the thing's middle. It burst into flames and fell apart, and Roland, Charlene, and the other witches struck the resulting pieces with lightning and plasma bolts. Blue light suffused the air as the thing burned away, then screams echoed through the canyon as the nearby crones faded forever.

Park chuckled. "This isn't so bad. I'm kinda waiting for the other shoe to drop. Doesn't seem like it should be this easy, does it?"

Dante replied, "Shhh, don't jinx us."

Another agent stepped up with a scanner. "He may already have, sir. I'm picking up an unusually strong and clear signal somewhere up ahead. It doesn't look like anything we've faced so far."

A dismal pall of fear settled over them as the man's words sank in. As mighty as their force seemed, they were fewer than sixty people, and suddenly it was as though the enormous canyon were preparing to swallow them.

Bailey offered to charge the new power source, what-ever it was, but Velasquez dismissed the notion. "I've got four guys here with prototype cloaking tech that mimics high-end concealment spells, and they have recon experience to boot. I'll send them to scout up there before the rest of us decide what to do."

The men he'd referred to nodded, fired up their cloakers, and moved out silently across the piles of rock. The canyon took a jagged bend not far from their position, so it was impossible to see much of what lay far beyond it. More crones were starting to drift toward them.

There came a familiar sound and a dim purple glow from off to Bailey's right. She instinctively put the sword behind her back, trying to dismiss her nervousness as she stared into the mouth of the portal.

The god who stepped out of it was not Fenris, but Loki.

"Well," she remarked, "I figured you'd show up sooner or later. We were finishing up an honest day's work."

The lord of mischief smirked. "I wouldn't know anything about *that*, but I'm sure you've been having plenty of fun."

She rested her sword over her shoulder. "Sorta. Let me guess; you want to talk in private?"

He confirmed her assumption, and the pair wandered off to an empty nook in the rock. Though pockets of specters were threatening to attack again, the mortal forces had cleared over a mile of the canyon, so there was no shortage of elbow room. Velasquez's men had brought extra field-generator poles to protect the territory they'd conquered.

Loki smoothed out his long black hair. "Without further ado, I, as the god of mischief, trickery, discord, deceit, and other such charming characteristics, hereby offer to further train you, Bailey Nordin, in the sublime arts of magic. Particularly the less obvious ones, which I doubt you'd have learned from Balder, though I suppose Coyote might have conveyed something useful."

The girl shrugged. "Both of them had helpful things to teach me. What about you?"

"There are a vast number of things I could show you," Loki extrapolated, "but we haven't time for all of them. I thought I'd start by instructing you in the *proper* usage of that little trick you learned from my son, Fenris, the thing about siphoning magic from powerful entities. Remember that?"

"Yeah." She grunted. "How could I possibly forget?"

He smiled and tilted his head back, looking at the witch-haunted sky as though admiring clouds on a sunny day. "I taught him that. I don't *particularly* want him to destroy the world as we know it, so I'd say it's valid for you to know all that he knows, if not more."

The werewitch bowed her head. "I accept your offer."

Before they began, she turned toward the rest of her allies, who, over half a mile distant, looked like bugs. She sent a psychic message to Roland, informing him that she'd be busy with training exercises for a short while and to proceed without her, though she'd remain here in case they needed her.

"I heard that," Loki chuckled. "I'm sure they'll survive without your help. Look, they even have shiny *sticks* that can perform the functions of basic spells!"

"They're only human," Bailey pointed out. "Cut them some slack."

While Roland, Velasquez, and the others reconfigured their base camp and plotted their next moves against the specters, Bailey and Loki sat down across from one another in the shadow of the high cliff to meditate.

The girl felt her mind expand as normal consciousness faded away. The world narrowed to little more than the space between her and the god of mischief and the growing mental link between them.

Then a ball of light, a pale and mildly unpleasant yellowish-green color, appeared in front of Loki's face.

This, he said with his mind, *is my magical essence. Or part of it, anyway. See it, feel it, understand it. I'm going to push it over to you, and I want you to push it back.*

Although it sounded easy, the werewitch had trouble at first. She hadn't dealt with disembodied energy like this before. It was easier to connect to another's essence when it was safely embedded within the being.

Still, after a short period of extra concentration, she was able to "locate" the ball in the astral as well as the physical realm, and she visualized the tendrils emerging to lock into it, as she'd done previously with Fenris, Freya, and Aradia.

Good, Loki acknowledged. *You've anchored yourself to a source of power that isn't tied up inside another sentient entity. Convenient, isn't it?*

Yes, she replied. *In fact, isn't this basically what Callie was doing? The witch who made all these ghost crones.*

In a way, you are correct. The trickster god's amusement was palpable through the mental link. *From what I can tell of her, she is—or was—not the brightest of individuals, so it's extraordinary that she stumbled onto such a powerful technique. Now, focus. Push the ball back to me, and then try to pull it away.*

Once more, the task was harder than it sounded. It took what felt like an hour before she could move the essence-pulse at will, and as soon as she had the hang of it, Loki began to resist her, pulling it toward him or off to the side while she struggled to bring it in her direction.

The god of mischief explained his reasoning as they strained against each other's will.

The idea, you see, is to employ deftness and subtlety in using and manipulating the energy of another, availing yourself of any power source you can find, regardless of whether it "belongs" to someone else, and if possible, using it without them being aware. If they object, find a way to trick them out of it, anyway. You find that morally questionable, don't you? Well, it's not something to do all the time, only when necessary.

Bailey had learned well that certain things became imperative under desperate circumstances, and she grudgingly admitted that Loki had a point.

They continued the exercise as he further detailed things that would help her perform this action on her own. She'd siphoned the magic of gods before, but solely in formalized, ritual contexts where she'd had the help of Fenris. To be able to do it on her own without aid would bring her up to the level of the gods.

It must become second nature to you, Bailey, he went on. *Keep at it, and try to draw upon my essence from different angles and directions.*

The perception of time was distorted in the Other, and the werewitch felt that a day or more had passed, though the activities of the far-off agents suggested that it couldn't have been more than a couple of hours.

Practice continued, the girl growing more adept.

Good, said Loki.

Then something changed. Bailey's link expanded beyond the disembodied ball of chartreuse light and tapped into the core of Loki's personal power. Some of his magic flowed into her. The bleeding-out process had begun.

She tried not to panic; she wanted to apologize.

I didn't mean to do that, she asserted. *I can give it back to you.*

Loki laughed out loud and spoke with his physical voice. "No need, though I appreciate the offer. Keep it as a small gift from me to you. Magic isn't lost forever. I will recharge soon enough, provided I don't have to fight too hard. Besides, as a deity of subterfuge, I work better in the shadows than on the front lines."

Bailey ended the link. The portion of Loki's power she'd absorbed, small as it was, had reenergized her; she didn't need more. She felt the excess bleeding into the fabric of the Other, but it dried up quickly, and the mischief-god did not seem too badly affected.

He stood, and she did likewise.

"Splendid," he commended her. "Far from perfect, but good progress for an afternoon's work. Allow me to walk you back to join your friends. They're reckless without you to spearhead their endeavor, aren't they?"

She shrugged. "They did pretty well without me."

"Perhaps they did." Loki took her hand, and they strode across the canyon's rocky floor.

Agent Velasquez came to greet her, with Park and Roland in tow. "Finished? If you're able, we can use you."

Loki raised a finger. "Why use her when you can use

me? Or both of us. I offer you a smidgeon of help before I depart."

Half the men looked uncertain. Most of them didn't know who Loki was, but they all sensed that he was a supernatural being of great power.

The trickster looked around. "Where is that adorable toy you have for tracking down concentrations of magic power? Ah, there it is. Please let me see it; there's something I'd like to point out."

Bailey nodded at Velasquez to indicate that it was safe to do so. He frowned but grabbed the scanner tablet and handed it to the black-haired god.

Loki moved his finger around the screen, and it took the mortals a second to realize that he was expanding the device's view and reach. "There," he said, pointing to an especially large concentration of pulsating light. "That is where you should strike next. It is not the heart of the problem, but plowing through it will clear you a path to where the actual heart is located."

Velasquez furrowed his brow. "Judging by all those weaker blobs," he observed, "there are at least a hundred of the eldritch crone spirits at that position. Bailey at full power can deal with maybe half of them, and I'm not sure about the rest of us dealing with the remainder without suffering major casualties. How are we supposed to get through?"

Smirking, Loki answered the question without delay. "Well, I'm a god. I can't fight your battles for you since unlike certain other deities, my existence doesn't antedate the non-intervention pact." He glanced at Bailey. "But like my son, I can conveniently use portals to chauffeur you to the right place at the right time. It's a touch difficult, but doable. Follow the gateway I provide and go in guns blazing. Have Bailey...what's the word you use? Have her *nuke* the specters and the spectral plasm nodes. Get rid of them posthaste."

The strategy he'd proposed wasn't radically different from what they'd been doing so far, anyway, so the agents agreed to it. As Loki summoned a portal, though, he turned to Bailey for an aside.

"However," he added, to her, "keep one thing in mind. Dealing with problems by nuking them isn't *always* the best solution."

He winked, then vanished into thin air before she could ask what the hell that meant.

Presumably it amused the god of mischief to have surreptitiously opened the new portal behind them all before he disappeared.

"Oh," Roland muttered, sighting it. "I was, uh, afraid there for a second."

Velasquez shook his head. "Everybody, move out."

Steeling themselves and taking deep breaths, the force fell into position and filed through the glowing gateway, knowing they might be plunged into combat the instant they emerged.

Bailey went through first, with two elite agents practically attached to her elbows, and after the brief disorientation of portaling, she stepped out into another area much like the one they'd been in. She jogged forward to create extra space for the people coming out behind her.

She saw that while they wouldn't have to fight *instantly*, there was not going to be much of a delay, either.

Perhaps a thousand feet away from them, a small army of eldritch crones hovered in midair, most of them at about head height from the human perspective. There were a hundred at least, possibly more like two. They moved in tight, roving circles as if patrolling, and, catching sight of the mortal task force, they set to wailing in unison. The canyon echoed with their screams of wrath.

It was easy to see why. A group of four of the gelatinous node-towers was clustered beyond the bulk of the specters, and another small force of the entities guarded them from the rear.

Velasquez raised his rifle and gritted his teeth. "Positions, *attack!*"

Roland threw up five slow-moving shields halfway between them and the phantasms, willing the arcane barriers to advance toward the horde so they blocked most of the crones' hasty and crude attacks. Streams of lightning, fire, ice, and plasma were absorbed, redirected into thin air, or deflected back at the horde, picking off nine or ten of them before the mortals had begun their own offense.

Bailey's blood surged through her body, pounding in her temples as she flung herself forward into the thick of the shitstorm. With her power, she had to create a massive wedge in the specters' formations, eliminating as many of them as possible in a short time so as to break their organization and allow her allies to mop up the leftovers.

She held her sword out, using it as a focal point for her magic. A bolt of lightning descended from on high to strike the blade and empower it, and the thunder crashed all through the canyon. The werewitch swung the sword straight forward and down, willing the vast forces at her command to act in conjunction with the strike.

A vertical sheet of electricity rocketed from the blade, cutting through the first half of the crones' front lines. Other crones masses were drawn toward the attack, circling around its sides and then spiraling back out into the horde. Dozens of the crones howled in defeat, their semi-corporeal bodies fading out or burning away.

Velasquez waved one hand, directing his men. "Move out! Left and right!"

The agents had drilled for a maneuver like this, and while maintaining a close enough formation that they didn't exactly divide their force, they nonetheless began focusing their attacks to one side or the other of Bailey's shockwave. Green beams slashed through sky and rock before finding their home in the eldritch phantoms, dispersing their magical structures and leaving them helpless.

Bailey stomped ahead, knowing it was far from over. More crones began streaming over the cliff, auxiliaries or reserves who'd floated in once the fighting began. Clearly, the intelligence controlling them was getting smarter.

Or perhaps it had put its more powerful servants closer to the larger mass of the anchor nodes.

The werewitch tossed fireballs left, right, and center while advancing. If any crones came too close, she slashed or stabbed them with her still-electrified sword.

She noticed something that disturbed her. Of the remaining phantasms, maybe one out of every ten was shielding itself or dodging with surprising agility. As her forces counterattacked, the smarter, stronger crones used creative magic, tossing out blasts that zigzagged or approached the agents from unusual directions.

Bailey caught about a third of the attacks, crushing them into an explosive ball within a sphere of shield-matter, then tossing them back at the specters, destroying another two dozen.

Others of their strikes got past her, though. A quick glance assured her that between the other witches' shields and the agents' well-honed evasive maneuvers, they were safe. Still, the fighting was going to be harder from here on out. Somehow she was certain of it.

Behind the werewitch, the mortals had reached the same conclusion.

"Damn!" Park exclaimed. "They're using half-assed tactics now. When did they learn to do that?" He aimed his rifle and fired, piercing the chest of one of the nearby crones and vaporizing it. The one behind it shot upward to avoid the beam, then descended toward them in an irregular pattern.

Roland trapped the specter in a small, controlled cyclone and tightened it so the creature did little more than rotate in a circle. Park blasted it and it faded from sight, screaming.

"My guess," Roland commented, "is that either the higher-grade crones are being kept closer to the main source of their power, or the power source is conferring higher intelligence and ability on them. Maybe both."

Dante groaned. "Well, that's fucking fantastic, isn't it?" He used a rectangular shield to stop two crones from attacking, then pushed it toward them to trap them against a shelf of rock. The instant he unsummoned the shield, another agent swept his rifle beam over both specters, destroying them.

They still faced several hundred, thanks to the hidden backup beyond the cliffs. Bailey realized that drastic measures might be needed if they wanted a quick victory without casualties.

She glanced over her shoulder to make sure everyone on her side was properly shielded. Roland and the other witches were doing their job, so she was confident they'd be safe from what she was about to unleash.

The girl spread her arms and a matrix of bright magenta dots appeared around her in a dome-like configuration, growing brighter and more intense in unison. They all exploded into arcane plasma beams that streaked out from Bailey's position in every possible direction. The sky was filled and slashed apart by them.

The beams ricocheted off the shields protecting her comrades, which increased their scattering and led to them searing through more of the shrieking crones. Dozens of them burst into pinkish-white flames as what physical forms they possessed burned and crumbled, leaving only the faint ethereal residue that the agents hastily dealt with.

Bailey noted that the new wrist-tanks with the built-in device to neutralize the crones' lingering essence seemed to be functioning well. She had to admire the speed and efficiency with which the Agency's research and development team worked.

With her plasma storm having obliterated all of the specters in their immediate vicinity, Roland and the other witches pushed their shields outwards in pieces and used them like battering rams to force smaller, more distant pockets of the creatures away. Bailey waved at them to herd the crone-spirits into a narrow crevasse in the rock above them, then she filled it with lightning and fire, fusing the melting stone and incinerating the entities.

They proceeded down the canyon, fighting and dusting more crones every step of the way. Though the battle was more furious than any they'd yet fought with the creatures, victory was in sight.

Bailey shouted over her shoulder, "Hold off the flankers while I take out the nodes. That'll dust them all."

"Roger," Velasquez barked. "You heard her!"

Dispersal guns held the crones at bay. The werewitch came up to the four gelatinous mounds, dispatching the few specters left to guard it with strokes of her sword.

She took a deep breath and summoned an airstrike's worth of fire, raising it from the ground rather than calling it from the sky. The light, heat, and flames channeled upward, ripping the pulsing anchor-things apart. Bailey kept the unleashed forces in a tight column directed up and away from her people.

As the nodes burned, flashes of light swept across the gorge, and the remaining eldritch crones moaned and caterwauled in anguish before dissipating into nothingness.

The sounds of battle, the screams of Callie's hideous crones, and the heavy breathing of the men and women who'd confronted them died out. Once again, the canyon was monolithically silent.

The mortals checked themselves for injuries before using field-generator poles to secure their perimeter. The lead agent then suggested they backtrack to join the current area to the part of the canyon they'd already claimed.

"Good idea," Bailey agreed.

She, Roland, Velasquez, eight other agents, and the three witches Bailey didn't know took charge of the short expedition, while Dante and Charlene remained behind, and Park supervised the rest of the Agency's men.

As they walked, Roland chatted with the trio of sorceresses.

One, whose name was Mavis, said, "I knew one of the girls in Portland who died. Never would have expected it was because of something like *this*. I'm glad we're kicking their asses. That can't happen to anyone else."

"I concur," Roland told her. "Really, though, it's only one person we're fighting. There's simply an unusually large number of her. It's probably for the best that she's barely recognizable anymore, since I used to know her, and, well...ugh. I don't want to talk about it."

Bailey decided to introduce herself to the witches. In addition to Mavis, who was from Portland, there was also Andrea from Tillamook, Oregon and Jen from Longview, Washington.

Andrea followed up the round of introductions with, "We've heard of you, obviously. You live up to the hype."

"Thanks," Bailey responded, "I kinda fell into it, as they say. A year ago, I never thought things would be the way they are."

Jen shrugged. "None of us did. Life isn't boring, though. Have to say that much."

They all laughed at that, though there was a sardonic edge to it.

Still, Bailey mused, *it's good to get acquainted with more people. I'm a goddess, but I can't become too distant from the average folks on the ground, human, caster, shifter, or whatever.*

Before the conversation could continue, someone interjected, "Look!"

Behind them, a man was hurrying up, having appeared from deeper in the canyon. It was one of the scouts with the advanced tech Velasquez had sent ahead to do recon earlier.

They paused and waited for him, anxious and curious about whether he was okay and what he might have found. He looked fatigued and concerned, but he wasn't injured, and the grim look of satisfaction on his face suggested he'd completed his mission by discovering something useful or important.

Velasquez jogged up to greet him, making sure he wasn't injured. He assured them he was fine, and he pulled up a small tablet screen that showed a digital light readout similar to the one on the main scanner the team was using.

"Here," the man began, "you can see the energy signatures of the crones, as well as the pulsating blobs representing those gelatinous node things. If we scan toward this grotto at the extreme far end of the canyon..."

Bailey and Velasquez leaned closer, with other members of the group peering over their shoulders. It was obvious what the agent was about to explain. The screen showed another energy signature, greenish rather than blue, and much larger. It overlapped the various node-blobs, as well.

"...we can see that this new thing seems to be sending out translucent waves, kinda like sonar pulses, to the other nodes. Given that it's surrounded by several of them as well as a shit-ton of crones, well, I'd say it's safe to assume that we've found our main target."

Roland tapped his lips. "Probably, yeah. I can't think what purpose it would serve other than to anchor and empower the other anchors, so to speak. And if it is the mother of all nodes, then once we take it out, all the specters will get vaporized in one fell swoop."

They glanced around; the phantasmal crones were starting to close in on them again, their numbers increasing.

Bailey smiled. "I like the sound of that. Nice and simple. Maybe not as *easy* as we'd like, but simple in the sense of, y'know, not being complicated. So, what do you say, Velasquez? One more big push?"

The lead agents adjusted his sunglasses. "Affirmative. Everyone, get ready to move out."

Fenris stood on a shelf of steaming obsidian, looking down at the flowing sheets of red and orange lava that was speckled with charcoal where it was beginning to cool. In every direction was at least one active volcano, and the sky, naturally a sulfur yellow, was the color of ash or hot iron where the eruptions were closest.

Here, too, was a section of the Other that was little traveled and almost unknown to most astral travelers. It was too harsh for anything to live here on a long-term basis. Fenris maintained a shield around himself in a broad sphere that produced a continuous shower of ice-cold water to buffer against the heat.

Footsteps approached, and the hooded man turned to greet his apprentice.

Carl took three more steps, then stopped and knelt. He, like his master, was shielded from the heat with a standard arcane barrier, though in his case, it was reinforced with cold wind rather than water. He was a youngish man, tall, athletic, and dark-skinned. His parentage was that of a changeling and a goddess, making him a scion.

"Fenris," he began, "I'm here. What news?"

The wolf-father nodded to him. "You may rise, Carl. Things are proceeding as planned thus far. The girl does not seem to suspect anything, though of course, we must be prepared for the contingency that she does. The gods of the council seem to have been idle. More importantly, I've stirred up the frost trolls, the dark elves, and the rock giants. All have agreed to assault the boundaries of Asgard while we make our moves in their shadow."

The scion grinned in a restrained way, then allowed his face to return to neutrality. "That is excellent. Unfortunately, I have not been able to locate Balder. Though I'm nominally his apprentice, he hasn't had much need of me lately, so I can't say what he's been up to. Do you think it's possible that he's spoken to Bailey?"

"Perhaps," Fenris admitted, his mouth a grim line across his jaw, "but let us not jump to conclusions. If he and Bailey have grown suspicious, that's attention drawn away from *you*, is it not? As soon as he returns, you will have your opportunity."

Carl cracked his knuckles. "Yes, master. With him taken

out, along with Freya and Loki, the council will be all but crippled."

The wolf-god stared into the smoldering sky. "It is imperative that the gods be crippled *before* Ragnarök begins. Too many of them still standing at the beginning of the End, and there is a chance we will fail. You must remove Balder, and soon. If at all possible, prior to the girl's death."

The scion acknowledged the order with a low grunt. "Yes. When do we expect that to happen? I will miss her, honestly."

"Truth be told," Fenris replied in a low voice, "so will I. In a better universe, she might not have needed to be sacrificed, but therein lies the heart of the issue. Her death will not be in vain. It will be the catalyst that leads us to greater things, a reality in which the stupid mistakes of Asgard will be no more. And she's nearly ready. Not long now. I will keep you informed."

"Yes, sir." Carl paused to refresh his shield. The furnace-like heat was wearing it down, and he'd started to sweat. "What shall I do once Balder has been neutralized?"

Fenris moved a step closer to his apprentice. "Rejoin me immediately. With the god of beauty out of the way, the two of us can confront Tyr and destroy him. That leaves only Thoth and Coyote on the council. They are not of the Norse pantheon, and there will be little they can do to stop us once our prophecies begin to come true."

"They're savvy deities," Carl pointed out, "but you may be right. The force of Ragnarök and what it represents ought to overwhelm any attempt at outside interference by them."

The wolf-father's eyes flashed with satisfaction. "Good, you understand the workings of Fate. Then we can challenge Thor. I will ensure that he meets us near the primeval waters where the World Serpent Jormungandr dwells. The challenge issued between us will summon the Serpent, who is destined to kill Thor even if it dies in the battle. All that will be left is us."

Carl chuckled. "As you said not long ago, a better world."

"Yes, Carl. You will sit at my right hand on the thrones we build from Asgard's rubble. We shall survive to rule over the unleashed hordes, running free in a world made clean again like a forest after a fire."

Fenris extended his hand, and the scion took it. "To the future."

CHAPTER THIRTEEN

The first wave of the gelatinous node-things had fallen. What they assumed was the true and central anchor of the horde wasn't far off, but the battle still raged.

Some of the crones were in a defensive retreat, spitting out magic as they tried to seek cover in cracks or holes in the walls of the canyon. Recalling Fenris's earlier lesson about creating hovering wards that could maintain defensive effects for extended periods of time, Bailey conjured two that would protect her from heat and electricity.

Then she coated them with reflective shields and sent them spinning into the tunnels where the crones had taken refuge, hurling blasts of fire and lightning. The deadly spells bounced off the spinning wards' shields and filled the rocky hollows with a randomized spray of ricocheting destruction. Crone-specters were reduced to smoke by the dozen.

Only a paltry number remained, and the Agency's warriors neutralized them in the span of another minute—another skirmish won.

Bailey, Roland, Velasquez, and the others advanced onto the scorched earth they'd cleared. None of theirs had died yet, but the seemingly endless numbers of adversaries and the increasing strain of prolonged, high-intensity combat were taking their toll. Three agents had suffered mild to moderate wounds, and nearly the entire mortal force was twitchy and fatigued.

The werewitch and the wizard collaborated on a subtle healing spell that would help the injured recover more quickly and with less pain or potential fever.

"After all," Roland quipped, "I had a decent knack for this type of magic to begin with, and I became a near-expert after getting sent to the hospital, what, like, five times in two months? I forget."

Bailey patted his head. "Something like that, yeah."

The rear agents brought up more of the field-generator poles to keep the crones out of the new territory they'd claimed while they rested one last time.

Velasquez waved his hand vaguely at the bend up ahead. "It has to be there. According to the scanners, we're almost on top of the damn thing, but we can't see it yet. One final blast fest and we ought to reach it. Only thing we don't know is, will it be as easy to destroy as the rest of those things?"

Roland shrugged. "I dunno. I've never seen anything like this. Most of my conjectures thus far have been *mostly* correct, but we're in uncharted territory here. It might be no more than a big node, or it might be the spawn of Godzilla and Cthulhu and able to defend itself accordingly."

The lead agent frowned, but the wizard just put his arm around the shoulders of his girlfriend. "Fortunately..."

"Yeah, yeah," Bailey grumbled. "When in doubt, make the goddess fix everything. I'll do my best, but I don't know what the hell's around that corner either. We'll have to see."

As they settled in to catch their breath while the agents recharged their weapons and checked on the wounded, someone stepped out of thin air, without creating a visible portal. The werewitch was not shocked to see who it was, and everyone else returned to what they were doing once they glimpsed him.

"Loki," Bailey greeted him. "Welcome back. We're getting there, but not quite done yet."

He glanced around. "So I have noticed. How are you doing? Holding up all right?"

She recalled the old saying, *"Don't bullshit a bullshitter,"* and decided there was no point in replying to the god of mischief and deceit with anything but the truth.

"I'm tired," she began. "This crap, all of it, is wearing me down, honestly. Everyone else is getting worn down too. We've had a couple injuries. Nothing serious, nobody dead, but still. We've taken out most of the targets, and we know where the last one is: right up ahead. I think we're gonna win, but it's been getting rougher."

Loki gave a slow nod. "Yes, that makes a certain amount of sense. I see you're all wise enough to rest before the final push."

The girl grunted in acknowledgment, but a thought occurred to her. "Loki," she asked, "I need you to be honest with me. In your, uh, professional opinion," she swallowed, "am I strong enough to take on Fenris as is? If I had to challenge him right this minute, could I beat him?"

The deity tapped a slender finger on his thin lips. "I am not sure. Gods cannot perfectly predict the future since elements of uncertainty always get in the way. However, you have a good chance. I'd say that if you continue on your current path, believe in yourself, and employ all you've learned and been trained in, Fenris would have a tremendously serious fight ahead of him. I can say no more beyond that."

He placed a hand on her shoulder—as his son had done, Bailey recalled—and looked at her with a rare expression of warmth and kindness.

"You know," he went on, "I think that just this one time, I will change my usual policy and tag along during the next phase of the operation—a slight bending of the rules, but nothing too serious. I cannot do anything direct or overt, but I can work around the edges of your activities and offer counsel. If you'll welcome my doing so, that is."

Given the nature of the mischief-god, something about him still rubbed her the wrong way, yet Bailey had no reason to believe he intended anything other than to help her at present. She gave him a wan smile.

"Yes, I will," she stated. "And I'm pretty sure everyone else will be happy to have another super-powerful being on our side."

They spoke to Velasquez, Park, and Roland, informing them of the situation.

The lead agent shrugged. "Okay, but it would be better if you worked with our battle plans rather than against them. Not that I mean to try to order a *god* around, but because we don't have as many options as you do, it's harder for us to adapt outside of the strategy and tactics we've planned and drilled in."

"Understood," said Loki.

Velasquez had Park break out another round of MREs as everyone sat down to eat. Someone handed a burrito-laden one to the dark-haired deity, who gawked at it, then sniffed it with mounting horror.

Bailey tore open her own. "What's the matter?"

Loki stammered, "Is this intended to be food? Do mortals truly subsist on such...material?"

Park snorted. "When we have to. Humans will put up with a lot of things to survive."

"Of course," the trickster muttered. "It must be bothersome to have a finite lifespan and have to cherish the years so highly that putting up with low-quality sustenance is an acceptable state of affairs. Perhaps we ought to distribute ambrosia to your kind after all."

Bailey stared at him, not sure whether to snap at him for being so snobbish or burst out laughing. He was acting like a fussy little girl.

Then it occurred to her. "You know, Coyote and Balder were both pretty big fans of regular mortal sandwiches. Cheesesteaks for Coyote, and a club with extra bacon for Balder. I'm partial to both, for that matter. This stuff isn't quite as good, but it's not impossible for a god to get enjoyment out of what humans eat. If you can't enjoy it, well, toughen up."

Squirming in place as he forced down a mouthful, Loki's only response was, "Speak for yourself."

Two men stood on a bleak cliff overlooking the dim vale below. One was broad-shouldered and wore a thick hooded coat, and the other was slender and dark-complected. Both were tall and looked formidable.

"There," Fenris said, gesturing to a castle at the far end of the valley. "We should not have any problems."

Carl smiled slightly. "Good. I'm not one to shy away from a challenge, but we've had plenty of those lately, and there are more to come. I'd say we deserve a day when things are easy for once."

The wolf-god led the way, and the pair descended a narrow path from the promontory while an icy wind whipped their clothes and hair.

The world to which they'd come was composed of frigid, swampy tundra divided up by low and craggy mountain ranges of jagged shale. The moisture in the low-lying mossy areas often froze, though snow seemed nonexistent. Black clouds raced across the sky with a speed that would seem unnatural on Earth, and behind them, the sky was a dark greenish or teal color.

Once they'd descended from the heights, the two found the winds less severe, though everything was still bitterly cold. Ice fog rose from semi-frozen pools here and there. They stuck to the solid parts of the earth and soon reached the castle, which was built into one of the foothills of the other mountain range on the valley's far end.

The structure was the same color as the hills, an ashy near-black, and it was carven with skeletal gargoyles. An inclined causeway led to the front gates. They opened when Fenris and Carl set foot on the stone path, and a guard or herald came out to greet them.

The approaching figure looked like a man, but not a living one. His skin was grotesque with the pall of death. However, he did not appear actively decayed; his form had been preserved in a close likeness to that of the living, though his lips were drawn back from his teeth in an eerie rigor-mortis grin. He wore tattered robes of dark green and black.

"You," the dead man addressed them, in a hollow, raspy voice. "State your names and your business in our domain."

Fenris raised a hand, palm facing outwards. "I am Fenris the wolf-father; you know of me, despite us not having met. This is my apprentice Carl. We have come to speak to the council of the undead, the lords of the draugar."

The dead face contorted in a creaky expression of skeptical mistrust. "What do you wish to speak to them *about*, Fenris?"

The tall god allowed a faint, nasty smile to suggest itself upon his face. "The prospect of overthrowing the gods of Asgard."

Understanding dawned on the face of the draug herald. "We have heard that there has been...unrest. Come with me, but do not presume to threaten us."

Carl smirked. "Of course not." Fenris waved for him to be silent.

The herald led them past the front gate and through the dim halls of the draugar's mausoleum-like castle, lit with torches that burned with green flame. Other undead faces peered at them from shadowed crevices until finally, on a higher floor beyond a broad spiral staircase, they came to the council chamber.

It would have been easy to mistake the room for a crypt since it was lined with dust and the corners were thick with cobwebs. Five monolithic square-edged stone chairs were arranged in a rough semicircle facing the doorway. In each sat a figure wearing robes similar to those of the herald, though both finer of cut and dustier from lack of activity. The five dead people, three men and two women, stared at the visitors.

The herald gave a bow, his movements oddly mechanical. "Great lords, Fenris of Asgard is here to speak to you about how the gods may be overthrown. With him is Carl, his apprentice."

The wolf-god and the scion bowed in turn.

In the central chair was a draug woman with wispy hair like tattered curtains and bluish skin stretched tightly across the bones of her face. She raised a thin hand and whispered, "Fenris, we welcome you today, though under normal circumstances, we would not. Word has reached us that your brethren in the shining halls can no longer suppress the peoples they have forced to the outlands. Is this true?"

"It is," the wolf-father answered her. "The frost trolls, dark elves, and rock giants have all risen up and assailed the borders of Asgard, distracting the gods and proving their weakness at my suggestion. If you know who I am, you should know that I bear no love for my so-called family. Their overthrow is my intent."

He paused here and there to answer raspy queries from the undead leaders in between repeating the essence of the speech he'd already delivered to the kings of the other monstrous species. They did not seem resistant to his pleas.

Fenris had dealt with the draugar before, though it had been a long, long time. Transformed from human corpses into immortal creatures of death by an eons-forgotten magical fluke or disease, they were simple-minded despite their relative intelligence. They knew little besides dark brooding or a primitive will to violence, and a desire to make all living things dead like them and feed upon their life essence.

"How," the council's head asked, "do you intend to deal with the more powerful of the deities while preserving yourself from annihilation? And what is your long-term agenda?"

The wolf-god kept his composure and glanced to his side. "Carl will eliminate Balder, who thinks him to be his apprentice. He is unaware that Carl works for me, in truth. Then the two of us shall confront Tyr, while we lure Thor into a confrontation with the world serpent. While this goes on, you and the other exiled peoples will launch your all-out assault. The divine realm will fall, and its tyranny will be no more. Then the way to the mortal realms beyond will be opened."

A handful of further questions later, the draugar's leaders' heads began to nod. They assumed that Fenris's own leadership of the cosmos would be largely a figurehead position, leaving them free to rampage across the worlds of the living.

The five dead figures looked at one another, then back at their guest. "We accept your proposal," said the woman in the central chair. "Vengeance against Asgard is reason enough for us, but the rest of what you suggest is...enticing. We desire prey. Deliver it to us, and we shall aid you."

Carl smiled and chuckled to himself with a mixture of relief and amusement. He'd been uneasy, but also hopeful about what they might achieve by coming here.

Fenris only nodded. "Thank you, great lords. The plan is a long time in the making, and we are guided both by prophecy and by the stupidity of the gods. All will go as I have outlined, so long as the girl Bailey Nordin does as she is supposed to."

Bailey and Loki sat cross-legged across from one another. They'd once more found a sheltered nook apart from the others in the rock of the great to continue Bailey's training and instruction while the remainder of the mortal force rested.

"Concentrate," said Loki, his sardonic face calm but strangely distant. The horror of having to eat lower-middle-quality human food had passed, and he was once again in full control of himself.

The girl, for her part, was too engrossed in the magical exercise to think about food one way or another.

They'd begun with a repeat of the exercise Loki had shown her previously, manipulating a ball of his siphoned-off divine essence. From there, they'd proceeded to more advanced techniques.

Loki had dismissed the ball, and they'd opened a link between themselves to allow for both the sharing and the stealing of power. It was like a compromise between what they'd done earlier and the method Fenris had shown her for killing a god.

The mischief-god said, "You will notice that at present there is a circular conduit between us; our powers flow into one another, then out and back, in a state of balance. This is what happens when a two-way channel is opened, but if either of us exerts the necessary will, it will become something else—a struggle for all the power between us."

Blowing air from her nostrils, the girl managed a slight nod. She felt as though the universe itself was passing through her, then leaving her empty, then returning. The magnitude of the forces involved was large enough that she had to maintain a mental state of calm and acceptance. Otherwise, she would panic, and the results might be catastrophic for either or both of them, not to mention anyone nearby.

But she managed. For now.

They practiced pulling magic from each other; a one-sided tug-of-war scenario in both directions. Then they opposed one another with equal force and finally began an honest struggle to steal as much magic as possible.

Loki stopped them before things grew too dangerous. "You seem to have the general hang of it, though in a true fight to the death, the intensity will be ramped up still higher. But knowing how this works ought to improve your overall abilities in the manipulation of magic at its source."

"Okay." She sighed. "Good. But why do I need to be

skilled at doing this? Is there a specific reason, or is this kind of a backup plan in case Fenris tries to bleed me out?"

The deity smirked and tapped a finger to his temple. "Trust me," he remarked. "I know many, many things."

Her face twisted into an exasperated pout, but, sighing, she opted not to protest. Loki was smart, and he probably had a plan. Furthermore, everything he'd told her about Fenris and the situation had turned out to be true. She had no reason to mistrust him. Besides his ancient reputation, of course. But it occurred to her that even an inveterate trickster could do the right thing when it suited him.

Loki raised a hand. "Begin again. This time, I will offer moderate resistance, and I want you to take as large a chunk of power from me as you can. Without killing me, of course."

The girl frowned but did as he said.

It was more difficult this time since her partner began his struggle as soon as the link opened. She had no time to "gear up" and get used to the bizarre feeling of so much divinity flowing between them. Heightening her senses while remaining calm, she rose to the challenge.

Then, as Loki's barriers broke down and magic surged into her core of being, the link abruptly ended. Both of them fell backward from their sitting positions. Bailey was shocked by how energized she felt, while Loki seemed exhausted and enfeebled.

They sat back up and looked at each other.

As had been the case during their previous exercise, Bailey blushed, feeling sort of like a distant relative had given her a large wad of cash for no particular reason at a time when the relative needed it more than Bailey did.

"I can give all this back," she pointed out. "You made the point, and I understand the process. There's no need for you to be endangered. We need everyone at full capacity for what's coming, don't we?"

Loki flapped a hand through the air. "Don't worry about it. You have, I'd say, earned the right to keep it. As I said last time, gods can regenerate magical power in much the same way that mortals can regenerate blood after losing a bit of it. I will be fine in a short while. Nonetheless, I am weakened for the moment."

Bailey looked at him through eyes narrowed with concern. He *looked* weakened—paler, shaky, and somehow smaller. "Will you be able to take care of yourself? Or to help us, for that matter?"

"Don't worry about me. As for aiding you, I can open one more portal that will be of use to you, but that's about it. I can get you in and out and offer advice. Beyond that, you will have to rely on yourselves."

The girl stood up and started to speak. "Well, I… *Shit!*" She staggered, and her head swam as she tried to keep her balance.

"Easy," said the god of mischief. "You've absorbed a great deal of power in a short span of time. Clearly, you will need time and rest to adapt to it. You're in no condition to plunge directly into battle."

The stubborn, gung-ho part of the werewitch railed against his words, and her mind searched for an argument, but she couldn't find one. He was right; she felt sick, confused, and disoriented, as though she was coming down after drinking a ridiculous amount of sugar and caffeine.

"Uuuggghhh," she groaned. "Yeah, think I'm gonna need a minute."

Loki slowly stood also, as though he too were ill. "You'll need more than that. Since time passes differently in the Other, I'd say you ought to go back to Earth for a short time and recover there. With the right, shall we say, *perceptual attitude*, your friends here will be fine and will only feel as though an extra thirty or forty minutes have passed. You will require hours, or perhaps a full day."

The werewitch didn't think she should abandon her friends when they were so close to completing the task before them. *But,* she admitted to herself, *it might be better to delay the last battle than fuck it up because I'm not operating at one hundred percent.*

She and Loki strolled back to the mass of agents and witches and explained their conclusions. Velasquez frowned, clearly impatient for victory, but he didn't want to risk Bailey falling unconscious in the middle of fighting or proceed without her.

"We'll wait," he said. "My biggest fear is that whatever intelligence controls these creatures is going to unleash them on the United States before we can finish wiping them out. We do well against them because we have the training and the tools. Same with witches and, uh, deities. The general populace wouldn't be so lucky."

Bailey took the man's hand. "If you get any sense that that's about to happen, send Roland after me, and I'll come back and try my best right away, no matter what. But if you can wait a little while longer, it might be for the best."

He nodded and gave her his blessing to go recover.

Roland embraced her. "Goodbye yet again, though I suppose it won't seem like very long. Take care of yourself."

She ruffled his hair. "Same."

Loki gave the mortals a nod, then, summoning what power still remained to him, opened a portal leading back to Greenhearth, Oregon.

CHAPTER FOURTEEN

After a few hours of lounging around the house, Bailey decided she was well enough to drive, and definitely well enough to eat.

"All right," she said to Kurt, the only one of her brothers who was home at the moment, "I'm gonna head out."

He pouted. "Aww, we were having so much fun lying around and watching bullshit reality shows! I guess I brought it on myself by making impertinent comments about Jacob's sexual proclivities. Next time I'll shut up so he brings me along."

"Right," Bailey responded. "You're growing up after all."

"Ouch," Kurt replied. "That was harsh. Does this mean I can legally drink?"

The girl pulled on her boots. "Not for, what, three more years? Or is it four? I forget."

They bickered for another half a minute before her youngest brother rose from his place on the floor by the TV and came over to hug her. "Be careful out there. Lately our town isn't a battleground, finally, but we all know you've still got some serious shit to deal with."

"I will be careful," she assured him, "and I will deal with it. But not right this second."

She left the house, hopped into her Toyota Tundra, and drove the truck into town, turning off Main Street toward Gunney's shop.

It was early afternoon, a warm but not too hot day with scattered sunshine. She parked out front and climbed down from the vehicle, pleased to see that Gunney had customers again. He and the new girl were working on an old SUV, and what looked like a Firebird was waiting in the proverbial wings in one of the other bays.

She waved as she approached. "Sup?"

Gunney waved to her without looking at her as he finished tightening a bolt, then turned around in time to see her a second or so before she grabbed him in a big hug.

"Oof," he replied. "Warn me next time, girl. You're strong enough to break me in half, remember?"

She let him go, smiling. "Sorry, old man. Anyway, not trying to interrupt. Need any help?"

He shrugged. "We're almost done, then we're gonna break for lunch for an hour or so. You can come with if you want."

She helped Gunney and the new girl finish with the SUV's rims. Then the new girl went home for the day while Gunney closed up the shop.

"I was thinking," he began, wiping grease off his hands onto a dirty rag, "of hitting up this barbecue shack they opened on the south side of town. What do you think?"

"Sure," Bailey agreed. "I'm hungry enough to eat damn

near anything. I'll tell you all about it, of course. There's that and more. It's been a crazy couple of days."

Her employer flipped his cap off to air out his scalp and hair, shaking his head. "I bet. Every time you come back, the shit I ended up hearing gets more and more, uh, we'll say 'improbable.' I believe you, though."

Gunney led her out back, where he retrieved the Cobra from its hiding place within the scrapyard. "Might as well travel in style."

"Hey!" the werewitch protested. "That's supposed to be my line."

They pretended to argue as they climbed into the old sports car and left the shop behind, cruising down the streets toward the new establishment.

As they drove, Bailey filled Gunney in on everything that had happened since they'd last seen each other.

"So, Balder came out and found me not long after you and I last spoke," she explained. "I can't remember if you met him or not? He's the Norse god of beauty and innocence, and he sits on the council."

Gunney sort of waved his hand in a circle to indicate that it was coming back to him and that she should proceed with the story. She did, detailing how the deity had joined her for lunch and then taken her to the southwest overlook for a lesson in swordsmanship that lasted until the following dawn.

"And," she continued, "then we went back into the Other, we in this case meaning me and Roland and the agents, since Balder left again. We went after the witch ghosts again, blasted the shit out of another hundred of the fuckers, took out some of their giant blobby mushroom crystal things that they use to anchor themselves to the physical world, and…"

The mechanic was rubbing his temple with the fingers of his left hand by the end of it. He tried hard, she knew, but she could understand how grasping what the hell she was talking about would be a challenge for him, despite his having lived in Greenhearth and therefore, around were-wolves half his life.

"Girl," he muttered, "you lead a heck of an interesting life, I'll say that much. I'm having trouble following most of it, but the universe is a bigger and more stupefying place than I ever would have thought. I went all over America when I was younger, but that doesn't seem like much compared to traveling to different dimensions and shit, not to mention you have authority in all this. You've grown into something beyond what anyone would have expected. I know I've said it before, but it bears repeating. I'm proud of you."

She grinned, enjoying the feeling of warmth that went down her neck and back at that. "It does bear repeating. Always nice to hear, especially since I know it's true."

"In fact," Gunney added, "since you're such a big shot these days, how about you pay for our dinner this time? I just paid you anyway—well, for what little work you've been able to do lately—so it's only fair. I'm a mere mortal."

She laughed and agreed. "Okay, fine. Technically I can conjure more money if I need to, but I'm trying not to get into the habit of that. Don't want to screw up the world economy by degrading the value of the dollar."

Gunney sputtered. "And now you're a fuckin' econ-omist too. Will wonders never cease?"

They spotted the barbecue shack up ahead, a literal shack that looked like it didn't have room for much food stock, let alone barbecue equipment. Its owner-operators must have known what they were doing since the place was doing a brisk business. A quarter of the town seemed to have lined up to try the place out.

Bailey watched the chattering crowd ahead of them, marveling at how strange it suddenly seemed to her. The people of Greenhearth were *excited* about a new place in town to eat besides the Elk and the sandwich shop. It was the most interesting thing to happen since the Venatori invaded.

Though most of the folks here were trying to forget about that.

Eventually, the mechanic and the werewitch found themselves at the shack's window. The menu was limited, so Bailey suspected that quality rather than quantity of dishes was the place's focus. She and Gunney both ordered ribs and steak fries, which they received in big paper cartons lined with wax paper, along with plastic forks.

They looked at the minimal number of picnic tables set up, and all were full.

Gunney sighed. "Dammit. Looks like we'll have to eat in the car. *Which means,*" he raised a finger and wagged it in front of the girl's face, "that unless you're feeling highly confident in your ability to eat this stuff neatly, your clothes are gonna have a bad day because you will not spill so much as a single crumb or drop of sauce in my Cobra. Got it?"

Bailey prodded him in the shoulder. "Yeah, yeah, you

crusty old bastard. I get it. Promise I won't blemish your pristine show car with my filth."

She was as good as her word and ate with the car's door hanging open, sitting sideways on the passenger seat and leaning out so that anything she spilled would land either on her knees or on the ground.

Gunney scarfed appreciatively. "Damn good barbecue. Hope they stick around."

"Well, they're doing plenty of business so far. Makes me a little worried for the Elk, but once the whole valley has gotten past the novelty factor of the place, things ought to even out between all three of our restaurants."

The mechanic laughed. "See? Economics again. Is this something Roland talks about that rubs off on you?"

"Nah," Bailey replied. "He's more into, you know, science and magical shit. I'm slowly getting him to appreciate all the technological genius that goes into motor vehicles."

As they drove off to grab a six-pack of beer from the convenience store, her mention of magic made Bailey turn her mind to how well she was processing Loki's infusion of power.

She felt better. Still weird, as though she were on an upper, but she was managing. Rest, food, and normalcy were helping. Soon, she'd head back to join her friends and allies in winning the latest battle.

But not yet.

Gunney took them to a lookout spot they'd discovered years ago—not a formal one maintained by the state or county, simply a part of the road up in the hills with a wide shoulder and a nice view. They sat and illegally drank alcohol in the vehicle, joking about which spells the werewitch could use to hide the booze if the sheriff or one of his men came by.

The day faded, and the man and the girl watched the sun go down. She hoped he wasn't delaying the work at the shop on her behalf, but if so, at least they enjoyed the wasted time.

"Okay," Gunney growled after a while, "that was fun. Thanks for dinner, by the way. Let's get back to the shop, and then I suppose you need to get back to saving the world."

Bailey's Tundra pulled into the gravel lot in front of her house. Roland and Agent Velasquez were there waiting for her.

She'd been half-dazedly musing about all that had happened and all she hoped could happen after things were peaceful again, but on seeing the two of them, she remembered her pledge to leap to their aid if need be. She tensed and snapped to attention.

Neither man looked frightened or hasty, though. She parked next to them and jumped out. "Hey. Are things okay?"

"Yes," said Velasquez, "but we're ready to move out. Are you?"

"Yeah," she answered him. "I'm a hell of a lot better. Needed time to digest my new powers, not to mention to digest some food."

Roland raised an eyebrow. "What did you have? We were still operating on MREs, so I'm curious."

She jerked a thumb over her shoulder. "New barbecue shack, south side of town. I'll take you there when it's all over."

Velasquez interrupted to hasten them along, and Bailey allowed him to. They knew there was important work to be done.

Roland opened a portal in the backyard and the three stepped through, emerging near the edge of the agents' base camp within the canyon. The force were all on their feet. The Agency personnel held their dispersal rifles to their chests, with wrist tanks fully charged. The few remaining witches stood beside them, ready to offer combat support.

Agent Park strode up. "Glad to see you back, sir. Bailey, you ready to go?"

"Yep," she informed him. "In fact, I'm better than ever, and since this might be the final push right here, before we begin, I'd like to say a few words if that's okay with everyone."

Velasquez adjusted his glasses. "Sure. We technically can't refuse any request you make due to the whole divinity issue, but since you're implying you'd like my permission, then yeah, you have it."

She smiled at the lead agent. "Gracious of you, and yeah, I could force you to listen to me, but I'd rather ask first and hear what people have to say."

He shrugged and awaited her spiel.

The girl cleared her throat and turned to the crowd. She knew she wasn't the most eloquent of women, but by this point, she did have a certain amount of experience with public speaking.

"Right," she began. "All of you have fought bravely. Some of you I met before on different missions, different battles. Fighting the Venatori, or in the earlier stages of dealing with these goddamn crone things. Others of you are new to me, but every one of you has done well. You know why we're here: because this bitch, formerly known as Caldoria McCluskey, wasn't content *only* to try and steal my boyfriend. Though she definitely did try that, since she's an idiot."

Low laughs went around the group.

"No," Bailey continued, "she's moved on to trying to steal *everyone* within the witch community. These replications of herself can only exist by sucking the magic and life essence out of other casters, and they've already killed way too many of our people. I say our, because I'm a goddess of both Weres and witches, and there are strong bonds of friendship between us lately. I hope that continues."

Heads nodded. She was the only lycanthrope currently present, but they all knew what she was talking about.

The werewitch went on, "We've been lucky in a lot of ways. We caught the enemy before they were ready to fight, when mostly all they have is these weak, dumbass, low-level clones. They're dangerous in a swarm, but we've kicked the shit out of them so far, and the fact that all we've suffered is, what, three injuries, means we're doing something right. We need to keep doing it, and we will."

Velasquez offered, "In other words, don't get cocky. I want everyone taking maximum care and observing all the prescribed instructions."

"Yeah," Bailey acceded, "what he said. We got this, ladies and gentlemen. Not even one of us needs to die here, and we *will* achieve total victory. All the witches in Portland or elsewhere who died or gave up their powers to create these abominations, we're going to avenge them and wipe this threat off the face of the Earth. Or the Other, close enough. Keep your eyes open, trust each other, work together, and we'll be back home in time for a nice early breakfast. Let's fuckin' do this."

Cheers went up, and her people pumped fists in the air. Roland smiled with a subdued appreciation. She might not have sounded as erudite as the people he knew in Seattle witch society, but she understood the red meat of how to talk to a crowd.

As the goddess stepped back and rejoined Roland, the lead agent stepped forward and went over the minutiae of their plan of attack with his men. Bailey listened to it, knowing implicitly that she wasn't expected to follow it, but also that she'd best be aware of what they'd be doing. That way, she could fill in the gaps they left, cover their asses, and, of course, act as their heavy artillery.

She also went over strategy with Roland, Dante, Charlene, and the other three witches so everyone would be aware of what everyone else was doing and worked toward the same goal.

There was one thing left, though—the wild card in their proverbial deck.

Bailey turned to Loki, who'd been lounging at the far fringe of the group, watching in silence. He looked marginally better than he had before she'd left but still sickly and enervated.

"Hey," she asked him, "are you well enough to participate? You said you might be able to help, but don't risk yourself."

"Oh," the mischief-lord countered, "don't worry, I'm quite all right. Mostly. And I do intend to help; I can just about manage a sneaky spell that will be of use to you. We don't know what to expect beyond that bend in the canyon, but it's likely to be far worse than what you've encountered so far, so I'm going to give you a little edge on the competition."

As the girl narrowed her eyes, wondering what he could mean, Loki extended his long, narrow hands, and a light grew between them. At first it was fuchsia-pink, similar to the standard magenta tone of arcanoplasm but not identical. It deepened and darkened to an eerie yet majestic purple akin to the hue of a portal, though with an odd burgundy tint.

"The hell?" Bailey asked.

"Ooh," Roland quipped, "a spell that's new to me. This ought to be good. Please don't do that thing where you say it's 'your little secret' or crap like that, Loki. We *have* to know what this is."

The deity smirked. "And you shall, this one time. We'll call it a special occasion."

Agents Velasquez and Park approached them, figuring they ought to pay attention to what Loki was up to, as well.

Addressing them all, the god of mischief explained, "This sphere is a concentrated time dilation spell. It will function like a bomb, but not a destructive one. When I hurl it and it bursts, it will cause a...what's that hilarious military term you people use? *Snafu*, that's it. It will cause a snafu in the space-time continuum, but for certain beings only, such as our friends, the eldritch crones."

Roland rubbed his hands together. "This is great. More!"

"Yes, yes," Loki chided, "I'm getting to the rest. The expanding field will effectively put the specters into 'slow motion.' For a short while, anyway. Spells of this type cannot be made to last long, or they cause chain reactions in the fabric of the universe that can be highly unpredictable and unpleasant, but once we're upon them, it will give you an initial advantage. They will move as if they're in a drunken stupor, while you are able to plow ahead to the main goal or destroy them at your leisure."

Velasquez, who'd been rather grim and humorless lately under the burden of command, grinned openly. "Nice! I'd say that's as good as a bomb of the incendiary variety. Warn us before you pop it, though. Will there be any side effects for us?"

Loki pursed his lips as he thought. It occurred to Bailey that being sapped of power as he was, his mind might not be as sharp as if he were operating at full strength.

"It shouldn't," the dark-haired god answered the agent. "It will make a flash and perhaps a mild sonic pulse, but nothing overtly harmful."

Satisfied, Velasquez had his men form up, and with Bailey at the head, they all marched toward the bend.

The werewitch breathed in through her nose and out through her mouth as she stomped across the stony ground. Roland walked at her left elbow and Loki at her right, the mystical purple glow of his time-dilation bomb casting the rusty red rock in odd wine-like hues.

Ahead of them, they saw that the angle of the canyon bent more sharply to the side than they'd anticipated. It was at least a forty-five-degree angle, maybe more, which made it impossible to see anything beyond.

Shit, Bailey ruminated. *I ought to fly up into the air and observe it from above, but I'd be abandoning everyone else if they get ambushed. If they have some seriously big guns waiting, I could be captured myself. Let's just continue with the plan as-is. How bad can it be up there? Those things aren't that tough.*

They came to the jutting shelf of rock that blocked off the rest of the gorge beyond the bend; all they could see were layers of naked reddish stone. There were faint sounds in the air, a low thrumming and a multiplicity of moans and whispers, but they weren't noticeably different from the noises made by the crones and the anchor-nodes the mortals had encountered before.

Then they rounded the corner and stumbled into a massive fuckstorm of shit.

Someone exclaimed, "Oh, my God!" and even Bailey drew in a sharp, gasping breath.

The part of the canyon where the scanners had revealed the main energy signature was laid out in such a way that anyone coming into it would suddenly find themselves in a vast, open space, hidden from sight until they were within it. For all her seeming stupidity, Callie had chosen to place her main anchor in the one place in the canyonlands that had the best terrain advantage.

And the broad valley was crammed with hundreds of crone specters.

"Loki!" Bailey shouted, "throw it!"

The mischief god didn't hesitate. While the droves of

the undead spirits around them howled in rage and alarm, he hurled the purple sphere into their midst, seeming to retain active control of it as it spiraled out. It burst in the thick of a good hundred or so of them, creating a burgundy flash like that of a looming thunderstorm, combined with an odd muffled vibration-pulse that set their teeth rattling.

Bailey could hear the effects of the spell. The shrieks and rustles of the horde decreased in both rapidity and pitch, as though they had reduced the playback speed on an audio file, and their mad dash to destroy the intruders became an absurdly ponderous crawl.

The girl produced her sword, raising it first and then aiming it ahead of her. "Forward! Charge!"

The entire force barreled on. Bailey swung her enchanted blade left and right, hurling waves of nuclear flame and storms of arcane power, while the mortal witches manipulated shields, wind, and circles of ice to protect themselves and their allies while buffeting the crones away from them.

Meanwhile, bright green lines of dispersal energy streaked out of the rifles of the fifty agents, turning the ghost-clogged sky into a net of contrasting colors like a laser light show at a nightclub or festival. Though the specters were all but incapacitated, their sheer numbers meant there was no time to vacuum up their lingering essences. The only thing that mattered was destroying their ability to resist.

As Bailey ran forth, she saw that Loki had collapsed against a pile of stone.

"Loki!" she shouted, slowing to a stop. The agents slowed too, covering her with their guns.

The slender deity looked like he'd fallen unconscious, but he retained enough self-control to wave a hand at her. *Go on without me*, the motion seemed to say. Bailey's gut clenched, but she had to trust him to know his own capabilities. She turned away and continued the charge into the valley.

With the first wave of the eldritch hags obliterated, their ultimate goal came into sight. There was no mistaking it.

Unlike the disgusting alien blue-black lesser nodes, the central anchor resembled a tower or castle made mostly of greenish crystal. It was close to a mile away in the werewitch's estimation, yet with its size and the clarity of the air, they could see it easily.

It had to be the equivalent of five stories high, and the crystalline structure was the stuff of pure, condensed magic. Vague shapes, dark within the bright material, swirled beneath the surface. It looked somehow alive. Bailey wondered if the movements represented masses of energy, or if they were the protoplasmic forms of new Callie-clones about to be spawned.

Crying out with the strain of battle and the shock of being consumed by a fight they now knew would be far more difficult than anticipated, the force of fewer than sixty people plunged into the center of the horde. Specters moved toward them as if drugged. Loki's spell had effectively removed their perceptual abilities from the current timeline, trapping them in another that was lagging behind, always too late.

However, as Bailey slashed, blasted, and burned her way through the hideous ghosts, it dawned on her that they didn't know *exactly* how long the time dilation would last. She doubted they could make it all the way to the massive crystal before it ended.

A moment later, the bizarre gurgling chorus of sloweddown howls sped up and rose in pitch, abruptly back to normal. The roving masses of specters returned to their full speed, and they were *pissed*.

Roland threw up his hands. "Shields!"

He conjured one at once and the other casters joined him, either augmenting his conjuration or adding their own on the sides, or both. Translucent barriers of deflective and absorptive arcane force instantly came into being, protecting the mortals from the sudden onslaught of magical attacks.

Bailey used her sword as a focal point to channel pure heat in an expanding surge like a giant flamethrower, waving the colossal tongue of fire in front of her to incinerate the maximum number of adversaries. She also tried summoning a meteor shower to rain down on the huge green crystal, but something seemed to be blocking the attacks.

They needed to get closer.

She turned her head. "Roland, I need you for a second."

"Uh," he called back. He'd been separated from her by a good fifty feet in the chaos that had ensued. "I'm kinda busy here."

The girl cursed; he was right. The rest of her friends needed him to keep them alive, as he was their chief expert on defensive magic.

She returned her attention to the battle ahead and found that the air was going dark as dozens of crones, packed so tightly together they were like a single entity, flowed between her and the others, moving at terrifying speed.

"No!" Bailey cried out. "Goddammit!"

She recalled her earlier observation that the closer they got to the source of the problem, the more dangerous and intelligent the specters were becoming.

The swarm that had ambushed them had positioned itself so that Bailey could not unleash a super-powerful attack to neutralize them all without potentially overpowering Roland's shield and injuring or killing her allies. The barrier he'd conjured was sufficient against the lower-middle strength blasts of the crones, but it probably couldn't withstand a nuclear blast summoned by a deity.

Suddenly the shield died, and the snakelike line of crones flew away. Suspended in their midst was Roland, his mouth hanging open in shock.

Bailey screamed and flung herself at the spirits, throwing bolts of lightning and plasma that picked off a portion of them, but not enough to free her beloved. She swung her sword wildly, forgetting Balder's training, damaging adversaries who came too close.

But Roland was gone.

Behind her, someone yelled, "Bailey! We need help!"

She spun and saw her remaining allies pinned down under the onslaught. The five casters were desperately trying to reconstitute a shield, while the agents fired their rifles again and again. Bailey summoned a horizontal wave of plasma fifteen feet off the ground that burned through the majority of the crones hovering over her friends. After that, they were able to get things under control.

But the majority of the horde still roiled in front of them, and it was advancing.

Loki appeared out of the crowd, staggering toward the werewitch, raising a limp hand to get her attention. She stared at him, her brain still trying to unravel what had happened.

The god of mischief gasped, "We have to get him back. Fast," his voice sounded strained and hoarse, and he was paler than ever. "Not only for personal reasons, but because they're going to *use* him."

The girl trembled with rage. "How?"

"As a battery," Loki extrapolated. "Stealing the power of witches was their game all along, wasn't it? But if that crystal is their primary power source, then having it absorb his strength will cause it to filter out to the entire horde. And he, while not on *our* level as gods, is a mortal caster of unusually great ability. By adding his power, they can increase their average strength to a uniform baseline level much higher than it is at present. Individual specters would be a match for individual mortal witches, rather than needing a dozen or more at a time to overpower a single person. Imagine if the Venatori were slightly less talented, but had attacked you with thousands of troops instead of mere dozens or low hundreds, and you can see why—"

"*Fucking-ass shit!*" Bailey burst out. "We have to get him back!"

Loki sighed. "Yes, I was getting to that part."

CHAPTER FIFTEEN

Roland's vision gradually returned to him. He almost wished it *hadn't* since he wasn't sure he wanted to see where he was.

Since the witch-specters had captured him, he'd fallen into a semi-conscious fugue state in which there was nothing but a vague and chaotic procession of lights and colors, hideous noises, dizziness, and nausea. It reminded him of the bizarre, fucked-up dreams he'd had in the hospital while drugged up and recovering from his numerous injuries over the last several months.

His senses came back, and the world around him took on a semblance of order. He was standing up straight, though awkwardly; his feet seemed to be braced on a small, irregular surface that could not support him. Then he grasped that his arms were raised and bindings were holding him in place.

His eyes made out the dark skies of the canyon realm, as well as the shifting translucent hues of the wafting crones and the emerald energy they'd seen surrounding the giant crystal.

The green light was coming from all around him, and from behind him as well.

Oh, crap. He tried not to panic. *Did they crucify me here simply to be nasty, or is there something even worse about to happen?*

He could still move his head, so he did, rotating his neck and glancing around to take in his surroundings in more detail. Once again, he wondered if it might have been better if he were still blind and insensate.

He was perched high on the giant crystal. His feet rested on an irregular protrusion of its surface, and his arms and shoulders, as well as parts of his torso and legs, were fused to it with strands of a thick, sticky substance. The stuff was a dull bluish-green interspersed with bright flecks.

There was another thing. A power or entity, difficult to identify but all-encompassing and weirdly familiar, was...inside him. That was the only way to describe it. He wondered if he was demonically possessed.

No, he thought. *I'm being drained. I feel weaker than I should. Part of my magic isn't there anymore; it's like I'm bleeding out. This crystal is sucking my powers into its core to sustain itself.*

It must have been able to hear his thoughts, or at least sense the general nature of his moods and feelings since it responded at once to his inner monologue.

"Roland," a voice called. It was not particularly loud, yet it seemed to reverberate across and through the air all around him; it was omnipresent and insinuating. It was a

raspy crone's voice, but something about it reminded him of an obnoxious young woman with delusions of class.

He swallowed; his throat was sore, and his mouth was dry and sticky. "Oh, hi," he shot back. "Nice to hear your voice again, Callie. Do you have a cold?"

"*Shut up!*" she snapped. He still could not tell where the voice was coming from. "You know what's going on. I'm going to win, and you lost. And I'm gonna *kill* Bailey as slowly and painfully as possible. She deserves it, and she definitely doesn't deserve you. At the same time, you're mine. *Finally.*"

"Oh," he countered, "I've been strung up for sperm donor duty at last, then. Why are my pants still on? For that matter, where am I supposed to drop the ol' seed? Is anywhere on the crystal fine, or does it have to be in a special receptacle?"

The glow of the crystal pulsed with an angry fire. "Ha-ha, very fucking funny," the hag's voice snarled. "I don't need your body anymore. I'm past the point of that shit. Since you thought you got rid of me—twice—I've only gotten stronger. I'm *made* of magic now, and since you're too stupid to use your magic the right way, I'm taking it directly from you. There's nothing you can do, so just cry into your chest or something. Otherwise, shut up and wait for the end."

The wizard snorted, though his insides roiled with the beginnings of abject fear and despair. He could tell that the witch had drained a substantial portion of his strength, so she might well succeed at her goal.

But up ahead, beyond a couple of rock spires and through the haze created by the mass of crone ghosts, he could see movement and flashes of light and hear the noise of battle. His friends were coming for him.

"The end?" he posited. "I think you mean, wait for Bailey to show up and finally kick your ass into oblivion where it belongs. This is tasteless and shady even by your low standards, Callie. If you're going to drain me—and in a way that I don't get to enjoy, sadly—you might as well do it right fucking now because time is basically up."

Once more, the light grew brighter and more abrasive.

"Okay," the hissing voice said. "You asked for it."

The sense of bleeding, losing something, having his essence pulled out of him increased and intensified. Not by much, but enough for it to cause an unsettling pain unlike any he'd felt before. It wasn't excruciating, but it terrified him. It suggested that when the process was over, there would be nothing left of him.

Goddammit, he swore as he tried to struggle free. But it was hopeless; his bonds were too tight, his mind too addled, and his arcane abilities too weakened. *I had to go and shoot my mouth off. And so my girlfriend—fiancée—saving me is the only good-case scenario. Bailey, I trust you.*

Bailey let out an animalistic bellow of frustrated rage. The sound was echoed by the men and women who fought by her side. Their courage, the efficacy of their weapons, their intelligent tactics—nothing was enough.

It was useless, she decided. As powerful as she was, she could not move fast enough to get past the endless swarms that filled the gorge, nor could she wipe them out faster than they could be spawned by the central crystal and the other gelatinous nodes scattered across the realm, which still produced the creatures on the side.

The only way she could take out the main crystal at this distance would be to create so much destruction that Roland would likely be hurt or killed.

Leaping forward, putting her head down and extending her arms in front of her, she dismissed all thought of herself as a woman and allowed the beast within to take over.

Her hands struck the ground as clawed paws, and her form grew and elongated while sprouting dark fur. A red screen descended over her vision, and all her senses sharpened.

Her clothes shredded away. She could reconstitute them later. The smaller, more convenient wolf form she'd cultivated would not be enough here; only as a full-sized monstrosity could she hope to triumph. The sword fell to the ground, and distantly, a part of her consciousness surrounded it with a powerful shield to protect it from theft or damage. The rest of her mind focused solely on charging ahead.

The lycanthrope barreled forward, surrounding herself with a profusion of curved and angular shields coated with blazing flames of arcane plasma. She was like a living battering ram advancing at the speed of a truck burning nitrous oxide. Specters in her path were destroyed, her advance tossed aside the ones that tried to get out of the way and failed. Others fled to the sides, howling and shrieking.

As the werewitch ran, she left bombs in her wake—

floating wards that would protect her from her own attacks, but which she set to detonate in flashing fireballs of magical energy.

The specters that moved in behind her or tried to flank her once she'd passed them crashed into the traps, their ghostly, distorted faces screaming in rage one last time as the spheres of burning destruction engulfed their forms and blotted them out. The horde parted down the middle as Bailey plowed ahead.

Trailing her was the small army of agents and witches, the green beams of their rifles carving up what resistance remained. The casters contributed bolts of lightning and sheets of flame as well. The mortals had, for the moment, abandoned pure defense in favor of an overwhelming offense.

Entire sub-hordes of the Caldoria McCluskey's incorporeal clones burned, disintegrated, and faded. A moment earlier, they had clogged the very sky, but as Bailey raged through them, they ceased to exist. Only their arcane residues remained, mostly invisible, immobile, and powerless.

As the air cleared before her, Bailey saw that one last line of defense stood between her and the giant crystal structure. She realized that it would pose a challenge far beyond what they'd faced so far. Callie had saved her most powerful clones for the most important job.

There were about twenty of them. They were twice the size of the others, and therefore twice the size of a normal woman. Rather than looking like semi-spectral apparitions of a humanoid crone in dark, tattered robes, with all the natural colors that would imply, these phantasms appeared to be made of rarefied arcane force.

They glowed brightly, the illumination of their pseudo-bodies shifting from blue to green and back. Their eyes were bright points of eerie cyan. Crackling bolts and sparks moved along the edges of their trailing robes or between their gnarled, pointed fingers, sometimes leaping into the charged and hazy air that surrounded them.

Bailey skidded to a halt about a hundred yards before reaching them and performed two supernatural actions at once. First, she shifted back into human form, surrounding her naked body with a form-fitting shield darkened to provide the same benefits as clothes; she had other things to worry about than redressing herself properly.

The second was to magically seize control of the slight shockwave of kinetic force and dust she'd created by braking and push it forward, expand it, and lace it with elemental and arcane attacks. It became a tidal wave of sorcerous annihilation, advancing toward Callie's elite guard.

But if it gets through them, Bailey told herself as she stood up straight on two legs, *I'll have to stop it instantly. Otherwise, it will reach the crystal...and Roland.*

It did not get through them, though. Bolts of power flowed among them, creating a shield of multifarious rainbow colors, though it looked unwholesome, like light reflecting off an oil slick. The empowered shockwave crashed against it and both were neutralized, leaving the twenty over-powered spirits hovering before a cloud of smoke.

Gnashing her teeth, Bailey extended an arm behind her,

hand open. Her mind sought the sword Balder had given her, and the blade flew to her from where she'd left it, landing in her palm.

The elite specters advanced on her, letting out echoing trills that were like nightmare versions of bird calls amplified a hundredfold. Bailey ran up to meet them, charging her sword with fire and lightning and the raging plasma of the arcane.

Up close, the entities were an order of magnitude more horrible to look at than their lesser brethren were, which was saying something. The grotesque haglike semi-decayed features, being larger, were more blatant and intimidating, and their wafting robe-shreds resembled the tentacles of squids or octopi floating in the black waters of the deep ocean.

Bailey suspected that getting close was exactly what she wanted to do. They were ghosts made of magic, the arcane equivalent of smart drones. They were not *fighters*.

The first two hit her with blue-green beams surrounded by spirals of sputtering pink plasma-lightning. She took the blows, absorbing and diffusing the energy, gritting her teeth through the intense pain and forcing a portion of it to the sides to assail the more distant of the guardians

Then she was right on top of the two lead ones, her sword cleaving into them. Their arcane structures were denser, harder to cut, but by no means invincible. The goddess' blade, powered by her anger and drive, annihilated them. Tremors went through the air as they dissolved.

She repeated the process for three more, tanking their

attacks while knowing she was losing strength and being gradually damaged, but eliminating her enemies in the process.

I can't do this for all twenty. It'd be a suicide attack. I need to be smart and survive this to save Roland.

She reasoned that the guardians were each approximately the same strength as a powerful mortal sorceress. Gathering her wits as she plunged into battle against them, she shielded herself properly, identified the nature of the attacks they used and countered them with hovering wards, and created thick walls of ice and fire to divide their number into piecemeal groups.

Operating on focused rage instead of the blind variety, Bailey gained the upper hand. All of the elite specters fell before her sword save four, whom she'd boxed off behind an ice wall, their only line of escape being across a thermal column that would incinerate them in an instant.

They probably have enough intelligence to put the fire out or melt the ice, but by the time they figure that out, the agents will have reached them and can blast them to hell. I'll have reached the big bastard-thing controlling this whole mess.

She charged again, encountering another wave of lesser ghosts. Their overall number had not diminished much. New ones were being created to replace the heavy losses.

Breathing deep, Bailey encased the crystal—and her fiancée—in the most powerful shield she could muster, then nuked the valley before her. Everything turned white, then black; she blocked the sonic boom and heat waves from traveling behind her and killing her friends, instead folding them back on the blast's original targets.

When the smoke cleared, half the valley was empty of Callie's loathsome servants.

But there were more flowing over the surrounding cliffs in a blackish-blue cascade of dark sorcery. Always more; the enemy's ability to spawn the things was seemingly unlimited.

Bailey turned to the massive crystal, which finally was close enough for her to toss a softball and hit it. *I need to end this right now. And I think I know how to.*

First, she jumped straight up into the air, the motion transforming into flight as she soared higher. She hovered at the same height as Roland, who stared at her in a mixture of relief and amazement, though anguished exhaustion was apparent in his expression.

"All right, dork," she told him, "quit screwing around." She swung her sword half a dozen times, deftly severing the strands of sticky residue that bound him to the crystal, and caught him as he slumped away from it. With his form over her shoulder, she floated back to the ground and gently laid him in the dust.

His mouth opened and shut without speaking.

"You okay?" she asked. "I have to destroy this thing..."

Gasping, he managed to reply. "Sorta. And yes, you do. Be careful, though. Callie. Her consciousness..."

The truth of Roland's words was proven instantly.

There came a terrible ripping sound, and before Bailey could strike at the crystal, she and Roland were forced back by a combination of a gale-force wind and an earthquake. They stumbled over the bucking ground.

When they looked up, the disembodied forces that had gathered had gained a body.

The towering avatar of Caldoria McCluskey sneered. "I won after all, like I said I would. I already had enough power drained from all those other people, far more than you ever suspected. I have Roland's too now, and I'm *back*. You're fucked!"

Bailey gawked. The creature before her was as tall as the crystal tower, and appearance-wise, she was a compromise between the awful forms of the eldritch crones and the original Callie, a curvy young blond woman who might have been attractive if not for the obnoxious expression of stuck-up anger on her face. Power swirled under her reconstituted skin as though she were a direct projection of the crystal that had allowed her to take shape.

She thrust out a hand, and a thick horizontal column of blue nuclear fire sprang toward the couple.

Bailey raised her sword and, remembering all that the gods had taught her, summoned a mixture of defensive and offensive magic that took the form of an oscillating white sphere with crimson and emerald light at its edges.

The two forces met in the middle, and the resulting thunderclap was so loud it shook the ground and made cracks in the walls. Bailey instantly summoned a sonic dispersal field to relieve the agonizing pressure on her and Roland's ears. Behind her, she heard the agents and other witches crying out and hoped they were okay—especially since she might need their help.

Nearly all her attention was focused on resisting Callie's incredibly powerful blast, and a sizzling white mass between them was all that was visible of the clashing of their extended wills. With the arcane energy she'd stolen, Caldoria was on the verge of becoming a deity.

Psychic ripples across the astral plane filled Bailey's mind with fear, doubt, despair, and revulsion. She knew they were only psionic attacks, but they would wear her down in time. The crude, stupid, and malicious laughter behind them only spurred an angry determination that the werewitch drew upon to resist the assault.

While pushing back against the continual stream of blue arcane fire, Bailey thought of Roland and recalled what Loki had taught her earlier. She couldn't use the sword to cut her apart since she couldn't get close to her, so she used the clash-point between her and Callie's magic as the central axis of a power-circuit, opening a channel to her opponent.

"What? What are you doing?" Callie screamed.

Bailey drained some of the witch's power and hurled it off to the side, where it became a flashing white wave of heat and light that engulfed and destroyed an advancing swarm of lesser specters.

"*Yeah,*" Callie added, "well, I can do that shit too, bitch!"

Bailey's teeth ground together. "*Don't* call me that."

She correctly guessed that Callie was going to try to steal *her* power and throw it at Roland. The arcane arm-wrestling between the initial blasts they'd created shifted for a second in Callie's favor as Bailey gave a few inches of ground, focusing on the conjuration of a basic deflective shield.

It saved Roland's life. The curtain of white light that descended toward him flipped back on its caster, and Callie howled in pain as the unleashed magic seared her reconstituted form.

Bailey held. She couldn't win yet, but she had formed a

barricade against the giant witch's advance, and her allies, the agents and other casters, were running up to join her.

Roland gestured at the colossal lead specter. "Shoot her," he suggested in a weak voice, barely audible under the crackling of the sorcerous battle.

Velasquez grunted, "Way ahead of you. Open fire!"

Fifty green beams struck Callie from multiple directions. She howled in pain and deflected a quarter of them, but the rest struck her, gradually tearing her apart.

Bailey's heart skipped a beat as the witch tried to take advantage of the magical conduit by cycling the dispersal beams back at the werewitch, but Bailey grasped what was happening and redirected them first into the air above them, then back at their original target.

Whining and snarling, Caldoria dissolved back into random clouds of plasma under the combined assault from Bailey and the agents' weaponry. Bailey ended the circuit, then seized control of the mass of collapsing power and forced it back into the crystal.

The agents stopped firing. The canyon was quiet, like someone holding their breath to see what would happen next. They all knew it wasn't over, and more of the endless specters were spilling into the valley from the surrounding mountains.

Loki staggered up as Bailey knelt beside Roland. The wizard's eyes were shut, and his pulse was disturbingly slow.

"Roland," she panted. "Oh, God. Is he okay? I can't tell!"

The god of mischief glanced down at the young man. "He's fading. She took so much of his magic that his life essence was damaged as well. Bailey, he's going to die."

The werewitch froze. She refused to accept it while knowing it was probably true. Operating on primitive rage, she turned toward the giant green crystal, determined to avenge his death if nothing else. The abomination before her would go down in flames or better yet, a mushroom cloud.

Loki said, "Remember."

Too many thoughts and emotions were crashing around in Bailey's head, but she tried. Something Loki had said...about nuking things.

"No," she breathed.

In her manifested form, Callie had been nearly the equal of a goddess, and that level of power was contained within the crystalline anchor. Bailey knew how to deal with goddesses. She sent out a mental astral tether, plunging into the green mass, opening it and letting it bleed out.

Into her.

The gathered humans watched in awe as a shifting mass of light resembling the aurora borealis in the northern sky played around the werewitch and the strange arcane structure before them. Power, visible and palpable, flowed from one to the other. The crystal's swirling colors dimmed, and it began to crack.

Then it shattered, falling apart in a shower of dull pieces and letting out a shockwave of translucent light and wind.

Everyone except Bailey fell over, unharmed but stunned. The shockwave advanced outwards, and beneath its initial burst, they heard a ghostly wail—the sound of hundreds of identical voices moaning in defeat.

When the light struck the eldritch crone-duplicates around them, they vanished, leaving nothing behind—no residue to be mopped up. They were erased from existence. Their cries died out, and it was over. The magical plague created by Caldoria McCluskey was ended forever.

Agents and witches staggered to their feet and surrounded Bailey, who stood straight and still, facing the ruins of the crystal. Loki gazed at her with mounting awe.

She had absorbed the majority of the crystal's stolen magic. The power contained within her was so massive it could not be hidden. It leaked out from between the atoms of her body.

"Oh, dear," Loki gasped. "Bailey, you have, if anything, over-succeeded. You are now more powerful than Fenris."

She turned and looked at him, her eyes blazing. Her voice echoed when she spoke, but its tone was sorrowful.

"I don't care," she stated. "What good is all this power if I can't save the people I care about?"

The lord of mischief gave her a sly look. "You can't?"

Bailey looked at Roland. He wasn't dead yet, but he was close. The loss of magic had killed him.

Fenris had only shown her how to take magic from a supernaturally-empowered being and keep a portion of it for herself. Loki's more recent lessons had included the sharing of power.

She sent out another astral tether, linking with Roland. The incredible might she wielded began to fade as arcane essence flowed from her to him. She gave him more than he needed since she figured she'd need all the help she could get in the final battle to come.

The wizard's eyes flew open, and they shone with

magic. He jerked in place, rose to his feet, and almost jumped in the air. "Whoa!" he exclaimed.

Dante burst into laughter as much from relief as from amusement. "Damn! We thought you were screwed, man, but it's starting to look like the exact opposite."

Roland twitched his limbs. "Er, yeah. Hell, I feel great."

Bailey closed her eyes as she closed the conduit. She'd given up most of the extra power she'd gained. Still, she had more than she'd had an hour ago, but not by much.

It was worth it. Roland would live, and her partner had attained a level of magical potency that was halfway to divinity.

Velasquez wiped his brow. "Mission accomplished. Let's get the hell out of here."

Park looked around. "Anyone want one last MRE before we head home?"

CHAPTER SIXTEEN

"You're going down. Your goddess mojo isn't going to save you *this* time."

Roland backed up his threat by hurling a massive bolt of lightning that flew at speeds the mortal eye could not follow. It transmuted into a small tidal wave, a flaming meteor, and a cascade of frozen acid shards in the span of a second.

Bailey laughed. "That's impressive, but the goal isn't to impress. It's to, you know, *win.*"

She parted her fingers to each side of her face and the deceptive attack tore itself apart into a hundred sparks and fragments, though none reached her. They shot through the air, bouncing around erratically but clearly working their way toward Roland.

He scarcely raised a shield in time as the dangerous particles suddenly shot toward him, but rather than just blocking, the shield folded over itself to engulf and digest the projectiles, then converged on Bailey like a giant coiling mass of impenetrable arcane barrier-material.

The werewitch responded by rocketing straight up into the air, and the grassy field around the older family farm fell away beneath her, and Roland became antlike. The wizard followed her into the sky; he wasn't as fast as she, but surprisingly close.

In mid-air, they traded blows with plasma blades and massive spheres of concussive force, trying to knock the other out of the air. Finally, Bailey tricked Roland with a basic feint rather than anything magical and walloped him with a kinetic blast that sent him hurtling toward the ground.

"Shiiiiiiiiit!" he yelled as he plummeted.

Bailey moved at an unnatural speed to get beneath him and cushion his fall. He probably could have done so himself, but she'd hit him fairly hard. He might have been dazed.

A moment later, two pairs of feet gently touched the grassy earth.

"Okay," Roland panted, "that's enough for today, I think. Since I'm not a frickin' deity, I'd say I held my own pretty well."

She hugged him. "Yeah, you did. Not bad at all, and you're definitely stronger than you used to be. You're a demigod now, I think."

He laughed. "That's good. It means I'm not marrying *too* far up the totem pole."

"Right." She planted a fast kiss on his lips. "We had a deal, though. Loser buys dinner for both. If you think I had an unfair edge, well, you're the one who agreed to the duel."

He pushed his lips out in an exaggerated put-upon

expression and thrust his hands into his pockets. "Awww, do I hafta? Fine, I guess. The Elk?"

"Sure." She hooked her arm through his, and they walked together back to Bailey's truck. Since she had to drive over the bumpy-ass winding road to leave the old farmhouse behind, she figured it was only fair for Roland to buy the meal.

Once they were settled in their usual place, with Bailey sipping an orange soda and Roland a cup of decaf coffee, they turned to discussing the broader situation before them.

"So," the wizard began, "offhand, I can't think of anything else we'll need to deal with except your soon-to-be-erstwhile mentor. Granted, he's kind of a big deal, but at least there aren't any other threats looming on the horizon."

He frowned, his eyes going distant as he contemplated his words. "I think there aren't anyway. It's possible that fucking Shannon will still show up and try to make our lives miserable, though I doubt on the same scale as with Callie. The Venatori haven't made a peep, either. We've maintained a good relationship between witches and Weres, and the agents are still our friends, mostly. There's a bright side to look at."

The girl chewed on and digested what her lover had said. "You're right. All kinds of shit have been thrown at us, and we've rolled it all up. But the one thing that remains...it's not exactly minor, Roland. Not only because we don't know what all he has waiting in the wings, but, well..." She stopped and swallowed a lump in her throat.

Roland sensed that she wanted to say more but couldn't yet, so he waited.

Ten seconds later, she found her words. "Fenris freed me, Roland. He saved me from the thing that was always hovering over my head like that sword in the old Greek myth dangling over the guy's chair or whatever it was. He and I have been through about the same amount of shit that you and I have, and for about the same length of time. Not saying I, uh, value him more than you or anything, it's just that I don't want this to happen. I'd rather have him as a friend than an enemy. A mentor, like I thought he was."

Roland's smile was sad and sympathetic. Her right hand rested flat on the table and he put his own atop it, letting her feel its warmth.

"I understand. You might recall that I was a touch suspicious of him all along, but that calls the true nature of the issue to the forefront, doesn't it? *It was all a lie*. He deceived you, and he's using you. For all I know, amidst whatever bizarre things go on in the mind of an ancient god, maybe he does sort of care about you, but obviously not enough to be honest with you. And, of course, he plans to let you die in his place so he can bring about something you've been trying to prevent, which is a total catastrophe for the people you care about and everyone else."

Hearing him put it that way, she felt the gnawing uncertainty that had squirmed around within her depart. Clarity remained where it had been, not to mention a low, bright, seething anger.

"Fuck," she growled. "When the shit hits the fan, I'll thank him for what good he's done. Then I'm going to rip his goddamn head off."

Roland leaned back. "I don't doubt it. Do what you have to do, dear. As always."

Tomi brought their food, and they ate. The conversation turned far more lighthearted as they joked about stupid bullshit and things they'd seen and heard the other witches and agents do or say during the long fight against the eldritch crones.

Roland forked pasta into his mouth. "One thing I am grateful for is that we're back to eating the good shit instead of MREs. Actually, some of them weren't half bad for what they were, but nothing beats real food."

"Damn right," Bailey concurred, biting into her hot steak sandwich and enjoying the way the juice ran down her chin.

They chose to walk home rather than drive, enjoying the pleasant summer evening. Bailey checked with the diner's staff to make sure it was okay to leave their vehicle overnight. They were fine with it as long as they didn't get so busy the next morning that they needed the extra parking space.

"Well," Bailey told them, "you have my number if you need me to rush over."

They took the long route along the north rim of town to be closer to the woods, though with dusk settling in, the mosquitoes were out in force.

Roland squirmed in discomfort and irritation. "Ugh, someone should spray for these things. Dear, you wouldn't happen to know the chemical formula for Raid or any other insecticide, would you? If so, I'll happily conjure a cloud of it to surround us."

"I don't, sadly," she confessed. "Why not make our own bug zapper instead?"

They collaborated on creating a ball of light that smelled like blood and was surrounded by a powerful electrostatic field. It hovered by Bailey's shoulder and buzzed more or less continuously as mosquitoes swarmed into it.

Roland sighed. "Why do all these rare and beautiful species of parrots keep going extinct, while mosquitoes, the most repugnant living things on the planet, are doing fine? It's not fair, dammit. As a goddess, I demand you do something about that."

She rubbed her chin. "I'll think it over and see what I can do. I mean, ecology and shit isn't part of my purview, but once all this is over—"

The air parted in front of them, and a wavering purple gateway filled the gap. Out of it stepped a familiar tall, broad-shouldered, hooded figure.

"Oh," Roland said, blinking. "Hi, Fenris. We were just talking about mosquitoes and parrots."

The wolf-god glanced at him. "Hello, Roland. And that's...interesting." He turned his head toward Bailey. "I must talk to you about an extremely important matter."

She nodded. "Okay, then. What is it?"

She was pretty sure she could guess.

Fenris hesitated a second, as though he would have preferred to talk to her alone, away from Roland. Neither of them offered this possibility; they simply stood looking back at him.

"What I have feared," the hooded man began, "is coming to pass. In my rovings around the cosmos, observing troubling trends and speaking to my friends and informants, I have come to believe that the End will soon be at hand. A great doom is being planned for us all. Someone wishes to start Ragnarök."

Bailey allowed her head to drop down a bit, and she frowned at the grass. "Dammit, Fenris. I was hoping we'd have good news for once."

"So was I, but we cannot control the course of great events beyond ourselves, except in how we react to them. I still do not know who is planning this, or how or when they will strike, but we must be alert, prepared, and cautious. It is coming soon, Bailey. There is no escaping the basic fact that we must confront it."

"Oh," said Roland. "Well, that sucks. I was hoping we might take a trip to Disneyland California or something."

Ignoring him, Fenris wrapped up his warning to the girl. "Be on guard. Our enemies will manifest soon, and it will be time to act. You will hear from me again, and it won't be long. I can tell you no more at the time. Again, be wary."

With that, he turned and stepped back through the portal he'd come in through, and it closed behind him. The dim amethyst light faded, leaving the forest in near-total darkness.

Bailey and Roland glared at the empty patch of air where the wolf-god had stood.

"Yeah," Bailey muttered in a low voice, "we'll be on guard, all right. And we know damn well that the real enemy will be revealed soon."

Fenris sat before the black reflecting pool in the dead forest of petrified trees and bloodstained weeds that grew from the cracked earth beneath a sky like rusted iron. He came here occasionally to rest and meditate, and to conduct meetings with his apprentice, who was slightly late. No one else ever came here.

At length, Carl appeared. Rather than portal in directly, he must have stepped out at a more distant point and approached on foot, so as not to disturb his master unnecessarily with his intrusion.

Fenris stared into the black water and listened to the footsteps coming closer. "Greetings, Carl. I assume there's a good reason for the delay?"

The lithe scion sat down next to the burly deity. "I don't think I'd go so far as to call it good, but yes, there was a reason. Right as I was about to come meet you, I sensed Balder on the move and decided it was worth it to trail him, at least until I knew where he was going. He headed back to the council's chamber. I don't know why."

Fenris nodded without looking at his partner. "I see. Well, we will find out soon enough. In all likelihood, they are convening to discuss the outbreak of attacks upon Asgard's borders."

"That's what I figured." Carl shrugged.

Fenris pulled back his hood and allowed the faint breeze to pass over his craggy face and through his dark, silver-streaked hair. The air here, in contrast to the place's visual atmosphere of cold desolation, was hot, moist, and somehow salty. It went well with the omnipresent appearance of dried blood.

"In the meantime," the wolf-father explained, "we must

focus on Bailey. She's grown incredibly powerful—as strong as I am, or very nearly so, which was always part of the plan. She must stand in for me and be as similar as possible, but she could pose a massive threat if she were to turn against us. We must act, and soon."

The scion nodded to indicate he understood. "Of course. She was never exactly a lightweight, was she?"

"No," said Fenris. "She's not stupid, either. I am beginning to suspect that *she* suspects something. She may not know the truth yet, but she grasps that not everything is as it seems. We must be careful."

Carl cracked his neck. "Indeed. But she won't abandon people threatened by a crisis, will she? The whole point is to distract her with all the chaos so she dies heroically before she realizes what's going on."

Fenris kept his eyes on the reflecting pool. "It will succeed if we are vigilant. There were always risks, but I have planned this for too long for it to fail, Carl. The gods have grown too lazy, stupid, and complacent. The injustice of their rule is coming to an end, and with it, this whole world, universe, cosmos, or whatever they choose to call it that bears the marks of their flawed design and inept leadership. *We* will rule. It's coming. It's happening."

Carl was silent for the span of three heartbeats or so, then he laughed softly, shaking his head. He liked Bailey, he really did, but Fenris had promised he'd rule at his right hand in the new world. "I can't believe it. In a good way, I mean. You're right. Everything's coming together."

Fenris turned his head to look at the younger man for the first time. "Your next move is among the most important—to isolate and destroy Balder. You are more than up to the task. It's simply a matter of getting him alone, where the other deities can't rush to his aid, and where he is caught unaware. When you leave this place, go directly to fulfill that task. Don't go to the council chamber since we don't want them to see you shortly before Balder dies, but wait for him. He will go his separate way, and then you must move in."

"Understood, my lord." Carl smiled. "Tea?"

Fenris waved a hand and a kettle and cups appeared, though he would take the time to brew it the mundane way. "Certainly. We may not get another chance to drink before the beginning of the End is upon us."

The Nordin family kitchen and dining room were the most crowded they'd been in a significant amount of time. At first Bailey thought "ever," but then she remembered that it wasn't too long ago that a small volunteer force of Seattleites *and* a Venatori task force had been crowded into the same place.

Jacob raised his hands before the group. "Okay, don't worry, I made the coffee, not Russell. No offense, Russ, but it's two o'clock in the afternoon. That's waaaaay too late in the day for your stuff unless everyone's planning to be up for the next thirty-six hours."

Kurt sputtered, "How do you know they aren't planning that? Shit, I haven't pulled an all-nighter in, like, two weeks or something. I feel weird without one, man."

Russell frowned. "I thought people liked my coffee?"

Bailey leaned over and patted her middle brother on

the shoulder. "It has its uses, don't worry. But we have people here who are virgins to it, so it's probably best we break 'em in gently with Jacob's. We can serve your coffee next time."

Dante and Charlene, sitting in one corner, whispered to one another and cracked up. Bailey could have heard what they'd said if it wasn't for the laughter, scraping chairs, clanking plates, and general clatter that filled the house.

In addition to her family and Dante and Charlene, Roland was present, as was Gunney. The old man seemed mildly self-conscious around so many people half his age, but he took it in stride and listened rather than spoke.

Besides, if anyone had made fun of him, Bailey would have been able to shut them up in a second with no more than a death glare. She was certain of it.

Jacob poured coffee for everyone who wanted it while Russell and Kurt brought out the food; they and Bailey had collaborated on a feast consisting of two roasted chickens, a double size green bean casserole, some macaroni and cheese, and a metric ton of mashed potatoes and gravy.

Kurt announced, "Admittedly, this is more of a Thanksgiving-type dinner that you'd eat in colder weather, but whatever. Nobody ever complains about chicken and fixings, right? That's the advantage of it. This reminds me, though, we need to get a proper grill. Then we can invite you all over for a nice summer barbecue in, say, January."

Chuckles went around the table.

Gunney spoke up. "I, for one, ain't complaining."

No one else did, either. Instead, they dug in.

The eating was fast and furious at first. Knowing the size of the meal that awaited, no one had bothered to have much breakfast, and they were all famished. Once the gluttony had subsided, conversation went around the table.

Roland asked, "How's Deanna? She always seemed pretty cool. And those other gals who were with us at the end, Mavis and Andrea and the other one. Sorry, don't recall her name."

"Fine," Charlene chipped in. "She had some family shit to deal with. She wanted to stay and help us, but she couldn't."

Dante nodded. "Right. And Mavis and Andrea and Jen all got home safely. Jen has good taste in music, by the way."

That set off a debate among the urban types about electronic bands, hip-hop, and the like as Bailey, her brothers, and Gunney watched with a vague mixture of distaste and amusement. Greenhearth was a town where people mostly listened to country and classic rock, and that suited them fine.

Soon the meal was finished, and the dishes were piled in the kitchen. No one wanted to think about their existence, though a debate about who'd deal with them would certainly ensue before long.

Everyone wandered outside. The day was mild, as summer was waning. They stood or leaned against the pillars of the house's porch or its walls, chatting at random and looking at the sky. It felt good to simply digest food in the presence of friends and family, Bailey acknowledged, and talk about nothing more serious or imposing than the goddamn weather.

But it was kind of boring. Whatever serious shit

awaited them all, sometimes girls, even goddesses, just wanted to have fun.

"Hey!" the werewitch announced, pitching her voice so she grabbed everybody's attention. "I think what we need to cap this afternoon off is a race. I'm gonna hop into my Camaro there, and anyone who thinks they can take me is welcome to try. We start at the edge of town, then drive east, up to the scenic overlook. Roland, Gunney, you've been to the one I mean. Whoever comes in last has to buy drinks for all. What do you all say?"

Murmurs, chuckles, and boasts went around the group. Since some people were dithering or hesitating, Bailey added, "I promise not to use my powers to cheat. Well, unless someone goes off the damn cliff, in which case I'll save them. Otherwise, it'll be purely a test of driving skill. Come on, you know you want to!"

Most people voted for a nap, but Roland finally sighed. "So be it. I hereby challenge you to a rematch for beating me at the magic duel earlier. You had an unfair advantage there, but if it's driving ability alone, we shall see."

Gunney laughed. "I'm up for it. Once again, I think you all underestimate me. No one can surpass me behind the wheel."

Charlene stepped up. "Oh, really? We'll see about that." She was turning out to be more of a gearhead than Bailey would have expected, and she nodded with approval.

Jacob raised a hand. "I'll participate if I can borrow a vehicle. Bailey, how about the Tundra? I know it's special to you, which is why I'll drive it as gently as possible for this being a dangerous, illegal drag race up a winding-ass mountainside."

The girl nodded to him. "Deal."

With the five competitors selected, they all piled into their cars or trucks and drove, nice and slowly, to the eastern edge of town, gathering at a pull-over location for semi trucks about half a mile before the road to the scenic overlook began.

Dante had accompanied his girlfriend, and he got out of her car to volunteer for the duty of formally starting the race, vowing to walk up the mountain behind them afterward.

Bailey snapped her fingers as they all leaned against their rides. "That gives me an idea. The loser should also have to go back and pick up Dante."

They agreed.

The racers got back into their vehicles, breathing deep, as the younger blond wizard checked for cops, pedestrians, or slow-moving motorists. Then he raised his hand, made sure he had everyone's attention and brought it down in a chopping motion.

The five hit their gas pedals. A quintet of vehicles rocketed up the road that led into the Cascades, engines roaring and with clouds of blue smoke hovering behind them.

Bailey was out in front, but not by much. Gunney, confident in his abilities, hovered right behind her shoulder and tried to nudge her aside, probably bluffing with the threat of damaging her prized car.

Oh, no, you don't, the girl thought. Two could play at that game. She veered slightly to the left, so the two cars came within an inch of scraping, and the older man cursed and disengaged. She knew he'd have something else up his sleeve, though.

Roland was in fourth place so far, but he passed Charlene partway up the road. Jacob held steady in last place.

Bailey tried not to laugh. *At least that means he's less likely to fuck up my Tundra. But if he loses, he'll never live it down with Russell and Kurt. Maybe he can beat Charlene or Roland if nothing else.*

In truth, all five motorists were pretty close, and there were plenty of twists and turns ahead.

The werewitch grinned at the black asphalt and blue void ahead of her, welcoming the challenge.

Yeah, this one's gonna be rough.

You made it! Here we are at the end of book 8, second to last in the series. Thank you so much for reading this far.

So, one of the problems with not being able to go hardly anywhere is you…well, you want to go somewhere. Today I sat down and started figuring out somewhere to go during the rainy winter Oregon gives us in February and March. Hmmm, where can I go without running into Covid quarantines that's safe for my health? Besides, we'll have a vaccine by February, won't we? I know I will want to be somewhere warm for a while by then, and I can write anywhere.

Hawaii came to mind, but that turned out to be kind of expensive for housing for two months, even though the flights are dirt-cheap right now. If you know someone in Hawaii who will put you up, I suggest you go.

Where else can I swim in crystal-blue waters and bathe in the sun? Let me think.

Canary Islands? OK, cheap enough housing. Decent flights through Madrid. Problem? State Department Warning, which more or less translated to don't go there even if they'll let you in if you value your life.

The Balearic Islands in Spain? Great-looking little village houses by lovely beaches…and the same warning.

Portugal…same

Sardinia and Corsica and Sicily, you can't stick a toe in the water, it's so cold then. Flight prices are decent and housing isn't too bad, though.

By the end of the day, Jo and Storm and I had looked through so many Airbnb listings that I couldn't tell the difference anymore and I'd run out of favorite tags in the Get Me Somewhere Warm in 2021 list.

I was also somehow tasting the cuisine of each country in my mind as I browsed, which made me very hungry. No decision yet. Stay tuned.

I always thank my advance readers and the proofreader team, the ones who read my stories after they are edited. Special thanks this time to Dave and Dorothy and Diane and Jeff for hanging with me through this series. They help make this book (and every book) its best. Couldn't do it without you, folks! Much appreciated!

I hope you enjoyed Bailey's and Boland's further adventures. They will be back for their final adventure in Book 9.

And if you get a moment, drop me a review, please. Those keep us writers going! We really appreciate it when a fan takes the time to do that for us, and for other people who may want to venture into our world!

Until next time,
Renée

I COULDN'T DO THIS WITHOUT YOU!

Thanks to my early readers, you rock!

Dave Hicks, Dorothy Lloyd, Diane L. Smith, Jeff Goode, Angel LaVey, James Caplan

The WereWitch Series
Bad Attitude (Book One)
A Bit Aggressive (Book Two)
Too Much Magic (Book Three)
Were War (Book Four)
Were Rages (Book Five)
God Ender (Book Six)
God Trials (Book Seven)
The Troll Solution (Book Eight)

Coming Soon
Winner Takes All (Book Nine)

Callie Hart Series
Thin Ice (Book One)
Cold Blood (Book Two)
Feelings Run Deep (Book Three)